A LIFE FOR AN EAR

Fargo hit the ground just as bullets flew overhead. He spotted a log, crawled toward it, vaulted over—and took a slug in the leg. Fargo gritted his teeth at the explosion of pain and the hot gush of blood. But he kept his hand steady on his gun.

A skinny man dashed from behind a tree trunk, and Fargo plugged him in the chest. A bald man suddenly popped up from behind a rock and fumbled with his trigger. Fargo beat him to it, blowing his head open.

"Give—up—now—Fargo," Tritt screamed out. Fargo heard the pain in the outlaw leader's voice. And the murderous hate. Yeah, it hurt like hell to lose an ear. Fargo just wished that he'd aimed better. Or that he could get one more shot at Tritt. Just one more—before he himself got gunned down.

Trouble was, Skye knew what his chances were as the army of killers closed in all around him. Zero to none. . . .

⊘ **SIGNET**

TRAILSMAN SERIES BY JON SHARPE

THE TRAILSMAN

#180

THE GREENBACK TRAIL

by

Jon Sharpe

A SIGNET BOOK

SIGNET
Published by the Penguin Group
Penguin Books USA Inc., 375 Hudson Street,
New York, New York 10014, U.S.A.
Penguin Books Ltd, 27 Wrights Lane,
London W8 5TZ, England
Penguin Books Australia Ltd,
Ringwood, Victoria, Australia
Penguin Books Canada Ltd, 10 Alcorn Avenue,
Toronto, Ontario, Canada M4V 3B2
Penguin Books (N.Z.) Ltd, 182–190 Wairau Road,
Auckland 10, New Zealand

Penguin Books Ltd, Registered Offices:
Harmondsworth, Middlesex, England

First published by Signet, an imprint of Dutton Signet,
a division of Penguin Books USA Inc.

First Printing, December, 1996
10 9 8 7 6 5 4 3 2 1

The first chapter of this book originally appeared in *Sagebrush Skeletons*,
the one hundred seventy-ninth volume in this series.

 REGISTERED TRADEMARK—MARCA REGISTRADA

Printed in the United States of America

The Trailsman

Beginnings . . . they bend the tree and they mark the man. Skye Fargo was born when he was eighteen. Terror was his midwife, vengeance his first cry. Killing spawned Skye Fargo, ruthless, cold-blooded murder. Out of the acrid smoke of gunpowder still hanging in the air, he rose, cried out a promise never forgotten.

The Trailsman they began to call him all across the West: searcher, scout, hunter, the man who could see where others only looked, his skills for hire but not his soul, the man who lived each day to the fullest, yet trailed each tomorrow. Skye Fargo, the Trailsman, and the seeker who could take the wildness of a land and the wanting of a woman and make them his own.

Wyoming Territory, 1860,
where blue sky, purple peaks, and golden sun
were riches enough for most,
until the lure of green paper
turned one man's heart cold black. . . .

1

He was almost asleep, stretched out on the sun-warmed rock and listening to the moan of the wind in the lodgepole pines and the burble of the stream down below, when he heard it. Or maybe it was too far away to hear, but that sixth sense he'd developed from years of living in the wilds had made him feel it. However it was, he somehow perceived the twang of a bow, the whistle of an arrow through the air, then the sharp sound of branches breaking. Not close, but close enough.

In one motion he rolled over onto his belly, the butt of his Colt suddenly in his hand, and peered over the edge of the rock. Twenty feet down the tumbled rock slope, a brook glittered silver in the noonday sun, its occasional calm pools laden with the thick gold of spring pollen. His keen eyes shifted toward the crashing sound as a buck plunged out of the underbrush and staggered down the bank.

It was a superb creature with taut muscular legs, a wide chest, a proud head, and many-pointed rack of antlers. The arrow in its ribs had sunk deep, almost to the feathers, and a trickle of blood darkened the tawny hide. The buck took a faltering step into the water and its knees gave way. It fell forward, then onto its side, nose barely above the rushing water. Fargo watched as the buck panted, then shuddered, and the dark eyes went blank.

Skye Fargo tightened his finger on the trigger of his Colt and glanced behind him to where the black-and-white pinto stood tethered in the thicket of shadberry, almost invisible. His keen eyes swept the rocks, the pines, taking in the high blue Wyoming peaks sparkling with the last of the winter snow. No one. Nothing moving behind him. He shifted his gaze back to the scene below, wondering how many Shoshoni were in the hunting party. Shoshoni could be friendly to white men if they wanted. But sometimes they didn't want. Sometimes they got a bit testy when they caught white men passing through the little bit of territory they had left. It was just better to avoid the Shoshoni if you could. And here he was traveling alone through the Absaroka range, many miles from any white settlement.

Fargo had just decided to slide down off the rock and retreat to the waiting Ovaro when a lone brave slipped out of the pines and ran toward the deer. Too late to move now. The Indian's sense of hearing was as acute as Fargo's. Any movement against the rock would be heard by the brave. There was nothing to do now but wait it out.

It was a Shoshoni—young, wiry, and muscular, and he moved as swiftly as the deer he had killed. With his fringed leather breeches, he wore a white man's red plaid shirt. His braids were wound with several feathers. When he reached the dead buck, he stopped and then stood for a long moment, as if listening. His piercing black eyes swept the banks of the stream and then the edge of the woods. Fargo's finger was still tight on the trigger as he watched, wondering if the Shoshoni sensed he was being observed, felt his presence. How many more were with him?

After a long moment the brave shouldered his bow and drew the long knife from his belt. He glanced around one more time, uneasy, then fell to the task of butchering the buck. Fargo relaxed his trigger finger. The Shoshoni was alone. The best thing to do was to wait and watch, unmoving. The job would take a couple of hours and then the Shoshoni would be on his way. From time to time Fargo took a look out behind him, just in case. But there were no other Shoshoni to be seen.

The brave made short work of it with his knife and hatchet, expertly skinning the buck and rolling the beast out of its blood-wet hide, cutting the haunches and ribs into sections, and making packets of the various organ meats. Fargo admired the brave's butcher-craft. It was no easy work to do fast, and even so it took a few hours. The buck's blood attracted a cloud of black flies that buzzed in the afternoon sun and the spring wind carried the smell of blood to Fargo's nose. When the Shoshoni was nearly done, he laid his bow on the bank of the stream. He brought an Appaloosa pony out of the woods and packed the meat onto a travois. He was kneeling next to the travois and tying the two hind haunches onto the pack when there came the sudden sound of movement from the bank of the stream just a few yards away.

The brave froze as a heavy dark form rose out of the earth from the middle of a tangled copse. A terrifying roar split the silence as the gigantic grizzly bear shook its massive head and roared again.

In that instant Fargo realized the brave had been unlucky. He'd slain the buck just a few feet from the entrance to the bear's winter den. The smell of the fresh blood had awakened the grizzly, maddened with hunger after the long winter's sleep.

The Shoshoni took a step backward, fumbled for his bow, and then realized it was lying almost at the feet of the grizzly on the bank of the stream. Fargo could see the brave calculating his chances. His only chance was to run and abandon the horse and the butchered buck, hoping the bear would be distracted by the fresh meat. Suddenly the grizzly rushed, an enormous blur of brown-and-golden fur, of long black claws and teeth. The brave took off, but caught his foot in the stones of the bank, hitting the earth. The grizzly, attracted by the movement, lunged toward him.

Fargo's Colt spit fire. In rapid succession, one bullet through the side of the head, then another, then a third. There was no chance for the heart from this angle. The grizzly hurtled forward, throwing itself on top of the Shoshoni. Fargo aimed carefully, then plugged the massive skull again. The huge beast was sprawled half on the bank and half in the stream, the legs of the brave sticking out from one side. The Indian was struggling to get out from under the dying animal.

Fargo quickly reloaded his Colt, then donned his hat and went quickly down the side of the slope, fording the brook in long strides. By the time he reached the grizzly, it was in its final death throes, its sharp black claws scraping the earth, a deep shudder racking its huge body, and blood pouring from its eyes and mouth. The sound of its roar was indescribable. Fargo had seen many a man mauled badly by seemingly dying animals and he wasn't about to be one of them. The bear, seeming to sense his presence, roused itself and took a swipe in his direction. Carefully aiming so that he wouldn't kill the trapped Shoshoni, Fargo put two more bullets through the bear's huge skull. The mountain of fur seemed to heave upward, as if the grizzly would rise to its feet, but it collapsed, lay still, and did not move again.

Fargo quickly wrenched one of the poles from the travois and jammed it under the grizzly, pushing upward. He threw his Colt onto the bank and knelt in the snow-melt of the brook to get a good angle. The water was up to his waist in an icy grip. The brave struggled and his bloody hands appeared, gripping the bear's fur as he tried to heave the huge corpse off himself. Fargo hefted again and the Shoshoni squirmed out from under the grizzly and scrambled instantly to his feet as he watched Fargo warily.

The brave had been hurt pretty badly, his right arm hanging loose and his shoulder bleeding where the bear had clawed and bitten him. Two long claw marks scored one cheek—there'd be a helluv an impressive scar. But if Fargo hadn't been there, the brave would have been killed, and they both knew it. He was a young man, compact and muscular, well suited for the hard life in the wilds. There was something generous and open in the brave's dark eyes. Fargo found himself liking the man immediately. He tried out a smile on the Indian. The Shoshoni regarded him silently and his dark eyes shifted once as Fargo retrieved his Colt and holstered it.

"Friend," Fargo said, remembering the word in the Shoshoni tongue, which was a lot like what the Utes and the Hopis spoke. At the word, the brave seemed very startled.

"Not many white men speak the tongue of the Snake People," the brave replied with a laugh of relief, referring to his tribe by the name the Plains Indians to the east used. "I am Istaga," he added. Fargo recognized the word for Coyote. This was Coyote Man, and indeed, he had a wide grin like his canine namesake. "My people live to the north in the Land of Noise." Now Fargo grinned. Land of Noise? What the hell was that? He'd ask later.

"To my people, I am Skye Fargo, the Trailsman," he answered. "The Hopi call me Cloud Man. The Navajo named me He-Who-Speaks-Fire. The Cheyenne call me Nightwalker."

"These are good names," Istaga said, obviously impressed. Fargo knew the importance of the ritual exchange of names to the various Indian people. "I have heard of you by many of these names. But I will call you Eagle-on-Wind."

To be named after the sacred eagle was a great honor. And Fargo was sure Istaga had come up with that name to commemorate the fact that Fargo had seemed to come out of nowhere, like an eagle from the sky.

"Let's get a fire going and your shoulder fixed up," Fargo said. He was suddenly aware of the fact that he'd been chilled by the plunge into the icy water of the brook and that the late-spring afternoon was turning brisk. Night would be coming in only a few hours. "Then we'll butcher this bear. I want you to show me how you got that deer cut up so quick."

"You were watching?" Istaga looked surprised. "You are quiet as . . . as—"

"An Eagle-on-Wind," Fargo cut in with a laugh.

Istaga laughed at that and they set to work. A couple of hours later night was falling and they were sitting by the campfire, having feasted on fresh meat, wild onions and herbs, and a pot of coffee from Fargo's supplies. The rest of the buck and bear meat was packed and hanging a short distance away, suspended by ropes high above the ground so night-wandering animals couldn't get at it.

The Ovaro was tethered nearby and Fargo had exchanged his damp clothes for some dry ones from his saddlebag and laid the wet contents of his pockets to dry out on a rock by the fire. Fargo had used mud from the brook and some torn fabric of an old shirt to bind up Istaga's wounds. The bites and claw marks were deep and they must have hurt like hell, but through it all, the Shoshoni hadn't winced. Fargo admired the man's courage.

Now, with one arm bound in a sling and his shoulder bandaged, Istaga used his free hand to drink another cup of Fargo's coffee. He smacked his lips and wandered over to the rock to examine Fargo's belongings. Istaga picked up a double eagle and held it up glittering in the light.

"This is what the white man calls money," Istaga said thoughtfully. "Good to get a horse or tipi. But what good is this little sun except to trade?" He held the coin up again and looked at it curiously. "Maybe necklace? But bear claws better." He shrugged his one good shoulder and put the gold coin back on the rock again, then poked at a pile of dollar bills, payment for the last job Fargo had done. Istaga looked up questioningly.

"That's money, too," Fargo said. "Good for horses or a tipi."

Istaga picked up one of the pieces of printed paper, waved it in the air, and laughed with delight. "This good-for-nothing? I do not understand white men." He picked up a dead leaf. "What if I decide to make this leaf good for a horse? Then I have money, too. But this leaf is also good for nothing." He looked at the stack of dollar bills again, shaking his head in wonder.

Fargo grinned. The Indians were always amazed by the idea of money, and come to think of it, sometimes he found it pretty unbelievable, too. Fargo took another swallow of hot coffee and watched as Istaga picked up another piece of paper. It was a letter. Even from across the campfire, Fargo could see the faint traces of ink that had been smeared and almost washed away by the water of the brook.

"This is money, too?" Isaga asked.

"No," Fargo said. He stared into the fire for a long moment, watching the waves of darkness cross the bed of hot coals, thinking of the note he'd been carrying in his pocket. The ink might have been washed away in the brook, but he knew the words by heart. The message had reached him two months back. And ever since, he'd been following a trail unlike any he'd ever tracked before. This time the trail wasn't marked by footprints in moist earth, broken branches, or crushed leaves. No, this time, he'd been following rumors, half whispers, suspicion, and fear. The strange trail had taken him through the big spread of Nebraska and Utah territories, and into the land called Wyoming, from one two-bit town to the next, from the shabby office of a small-town banker to the tawdry glitter of a high-class bordello. Two months on this curious trail, and all the time they'd been one step ahead of him. But now he felt like he was closing in on them. Yes, he'd have them cornered soon, the men he was chasing. Just a few more days, maybe tomorrow. And he'd find the man called Doug Simpkinson, the man who was waiting for him in Starkill. And together the two of them would do what had to be done.

He felt Istaga's gaze on him and he snapped out of his reverie. "No, that's not money," he said again.

"That's because the water took away the magic marks," Istaga said, muttering to himself. He carefully replaced the letter on the rock and looked down at the pile of dollar bills. "That is how white men know what is money."

Fargo smiled to himself at the Indian's logic. Istaga came closer to the fire and stirred it with a long stick. The sparks rose like tiny comets. A great horned owl gave five low hoots off in the distance. In the cool night, the stars seemed close enough to touch.

"Where are the hunting lands for your tribe?" Fargo asked. "Where is this place you call the Land of Noise?"

In answer, Istaga used the long stick to draw shapes in the earth by the campfire. Fargo recognized the shape of the Wind River, the Absaroka range, and the Bighorn River. Istaga finally put the point of the stick at a place to the north.

"Home," the Shoshoni said.

Fargo knew the place. Most white men called it Colter's Hell after the tall Virginian John Colter, who had trekked all alone through the area back in 1807 and reported back that the land there was filled with rivers that boiled and hillocks that spit great fountains of water and valleys that bubbled like cauldrons. Most white men didn't believe Colter's stories and very few had had the courage to go and see for themselves. But Fargo had crossed through the area once, long years ago. He'd been in a hurry that time, riding for his life with a bunch of enraged Blackfeet on his tail, but he'd seen enough of Colter's Hell to know that John Colter had been telling the truth. The land there was as strange and mysterious as any he'd ever seen. And remembering the hissing and gurgling, he understood why the Shoshoni called the place Land of Noise.

"No white men there," Istaga said. "Last place now with no white men."

Fargo heard the note of painful resignation in the brave's words. Yes, it was true. Every year the prairie schooners came from the East, long lines of white-topped wagons bringing more settlers and homesteaders and ranchers who stopped somewhere and started cutting up the land, plowing and planting, building towns and roads and fences. The West was a helluva big place, but a man had to be blind not to see that one day all of it was going to get filled up with white people. And Indians weren't blind. Every wagon brought them more trouble, another meaningless treaty, and less land. The territory called Colter's Hell, far from the mountain passes leading to Oregon and almost inaccessible among the formidable peaks, was one of the few places left that white men hadn't tried to lay claim to. Not yet, anyway.

Fargo rose and suggested they turn in. In a few minutes more they were rolled up in their blankets. Fargo lay for a long time looking into the embers and thinking of the strange trail he was following.

By dawn, they had struck camp and the horses were loaded, the travois packed with the bundled meat. Istaga tried to get Fargo to take some of the fresh meat for himself, but he refused all but a day's supply. Istaga was heading north, a half day's ride to the Land of Noise, and Fargo's trail led him due south to a little town called Starkill near the jagged Teton peaks. As the sun tinged the tops of the snowy peaks pink, they led their horses along the bank of the brook until they intersected the north to south trail. There, Fargo raised his hand in a silent gesture and Istaga did the same. Then the brave glanced up into the sky, grinned his coyote grin, and pointed upward. Fargo saw a lone eagle flying high in the clear blue air. They nodded a farewell and Fargo turned south with some regret. He'd met a lot of men while riding out in the West alone, Fargo thought, and Istaga the Coyote Man was one he'd have been happy to hunt with and ride with for a time.

It was a day's easy travel down to the town of Starkill. The big-sky country of Wyoming Territory sped by beneath the pounding hooves of the powerful black-and-white pinto. The old trapper's trail arched up and down over the foothills of the Absaroka range, through stands of lodgepole pines and stretches of dense scrub oak where green leaves were just unfolding in the warm spring air. The larks were reveling in the branches and the land was full of big game—deer, elk, and moose. Far to the east, beyond his sight, across the high prairie, ran the Bighorn River swollen with fresh snowmelt. To the west, the range of snowy peaks pushed their heads against the blue sky. Hour after hour the Trailsman rode, sometimes pausing to rest and water the Ovaro or stopping at a rise to survey the land ahead of him, to look for anything or anyone moving across the land.

Yeah, they were out there somewhere ahead of him. The men he'd been tracking for two long wearying months. Dangerous men, armed to the teeth, a good two dozen, as near as he could tell. And when he caught up to them, he wanted it to be a surprise. For them, not for him.

Fifteen miles north of Starkill, he stopped on a high ridge to scout out the pine forest in the valley below. The sun had slipped below a gray bank of clouds that hung low above the jagged fangs of the Teton range. Then he saw it. His keen eyes were drawn to a movement. Something in a small yellow meadow that gleamed among the dark trees. Yes, there it was again. Riders crossing the open space, a good two miles away.

Fargo eased the Ovaro forward, guiding it off the trail to slip in among the dark trunks, moving forward at a quiet walk. The going was slow, but he knew right where they'd be. A few minutes later he heard the shouts of men, a cackle of laughter, and a sharp cry. They were just ahead. Fargo halted the pinto and slid down, gliding forward on foot, silent as a snake over the thick carpet of pine needles, eyes and ears alert.

The shouting and laughter grew louder, along with the whinny of a horse echoing through the forest. Movement ahead. Horses and three men standing guard, wary, looking out into the trees, their rifles at the ready. They were being damn careful, he could see that. He shrank back and took a wide circle through the trees, approaching from the other side. He wished he had hooked up with Doug Simpkinson already—hell, there wasn't much he could do alone. He slowly circled in again and saw more guards, a line of watchful men. But beyond them, through the trees, he could spot a crowd of other men. With all those men on guard, it was impossible to get closer or to see what they were up to. There was shouting, but he was too far away to make out the words. Then came the sound of another man's shout of anger, defiance, and—yes—fear. A roar of raucous laughter, the pop of three gunshots in quick succession. Fargo swore softly to himself, fury rising in him. There wasn't a damn thing he could do against two dozen men. And whoever had just been murdered—and he had no doubt that's what had happened there among the dense tree trunks—it was too late now to save him. He waited for another twenty minutes, hoping the men would move out so he could slip in and see what had happened. But then he saw the rising smoke of a campfire and realized the men were going to stay there the night.

Fargo backed away, melted into the shadows of the forest, and returned to where the Ovaro waited. He mounted, sat for a moment listening to the distant sounds of the men, uttered a silent curse, and rode back to the trail. Yeah, it was them all right. The men he'd been seeking. His fists tightened on the reins until his knuckles grew white and his fingers hurt. He noticed and loosened them, pushing his fury deep into himself, storing it up for the time when he'd get his revenge. It would be soon. And it would be sweet.

On the final stretch on the trail into Starkill, the sun

slipped out from beneath the thick clouds and hung over the peaks in a blaze of golden glory. Fargo stopped to admire the spectacular sunset, splashed with scarlet, fiery apricot, and burnished bronze. He was looking westward across a grassy meadow pocked with wild-flowers when a puff of white smoke rose up from just over the lip of a hill, as if somebody—somebody not very good at it—had just started a campfire. Fargo started to move on, but then thought of the desperate men he'd left a few miles behind him in the forest and what they might to do anybody they caught out in the open. The town of Starkill was just two miles down the road. Why the hell was somebody camping out here when they could get into town?

Fargo cantered across the meadow as the colors in the sky above deepened and grew richer by the minute—one of the most beautiful sunsets he'd ever seen, and he'd seen some beauts.

As Fargo came up over the top of the hill, he laughed out loud at what he saw. There, an old man with a long white beard and wearing a black beret stood in front of an easel that held a square of canvas showing a half-finished picture of the sunset. With one hand the old man held a round wooden palette daubed with bright colors and with the other he brandished a long brush.

Nearby was a badly staked canvas tent that Fargo was sure would collapse at a mere gust of night breeze. Two broken-down nags were tied to a bush so loosely they could pull away at the slightest scare. A lithe figure in a cherry-red dress knelt over the smoking campfire, her face hidden from his gaze by a wide straw hat with a bunch of just-picked wildflowers on top. She was laying green branches over the fire, from which white smoke was rising in billows.

At the sound of Fargo's laugh and the creak of the saddle, the woman looked up, and in an instant he took in a host of impressions. She was beautiful, her thick auburn hair falling in soft waves over her shoulders to her waist, her lips rosy against her pale skin, eyes blue as clear sky. The high collar and long sleeves of her dress couldn't disguise her slender figure, her high full breasts, and narrow waist. But she was no mere girl, and in her expression was a mixture of innocence and a long-carried burden, something that weighed her down. He guessed her age at about thirty and noticed she wasn't wearing a wedding ring. A nice-looking woman like her should have settled down long ago. He wondered what her story was.

Fargo dismounted and walked toward her. She stood up, pine branches in hand. The old man didn't seem to take any notice of his arrival, but continued to hurriedly daub paint onto the canvas as if to capture the sunset before it faded away.

"You trying to make a smoke signal?" Fargo asked her, nodding toward the smoking fire.

"Just a campfire," she said, blushing.

Fargo bent down and removed the green boughs from the tiny fire, replacing them with some dry grass and branches. In a moment it blazed up, almost smokeless.

"Oh, that's better," she said, flashing him a smile. "Thank you. My name's Bethany. That's my pa, Asa. Asa—Dalrimple." She gestured to the old man, who remained engrossed in his painting. Asa waved his brush over his shoulder, indicating he was aware of the new arrival but couldn't stop painting or take his eyes off the sunset. Bethany shifted from foot to foot nervously.

Yeah, she should be nervous, Fargo thought. He could be anybody coming upon them in the middle of the meadow. The two of them were the greenest tenderhorns he'd ever seen camping out in the West. Sitting ducks for whatever kind of trouble might come along, whether from nature or from other men.

"My name's Skye Fargo," he said as he extended his hand.

She shyly took it, her delicate hand warm in his for just a moment. "Skye Fargo," she said. "What a nice name." Unlike most people in the West, she didn't recognize his name, hadn't heard the stories that were told throughout the territories. From the paleness of her skin and her clothing, Fargo figured she'd spent her life back East.

"I don't mean to pry, but are you planning on spending the night here?"

"We're heading toward a town called Starkill," Bethany answered. "I guess we'll get there tomorrow."

"Just some advice from a stranger," Fargo said. "I'd get into town tonight, find a good hotel room. Camping in the wilds is fine when you know what you're doing." He lightly toed the wobbly stake that was holding one corner of the tent, and at the slight pressure it pulled loose and the tent collapsed.

Bethany's mouth formed a silent *oh*. Her blue eyes followed him as he approached the two old nags and retied them more securely to a chokecherry bush.

"Voilà!" Asa Dalrimple's voice rang out as he stepped back from the canvas and twirled his brush in the air.

Fargo walked over to take a look. It was a helluva nice picture. The sunset had faded to red and gray above the Tetons, but on the rectangle of canvas Asa had managed to capture it in all its glory. The old man had gotten the colors just right and the tall snowy peaks that seemed to gnaw at the clouds.

"You interested in buying a painting?" Dalrimple asked as he started cleaning his brush with a rag full of pungent turpentine.

"If I was, I'd buy this one," Fargo answered truthfully. It was damn good. "But I've got no place to hang it. And besides, I get a free sunset every evening. Every night a different picture."

"Talk like that would put us artists out of business," Dalrimple said with a laugh, wiping his palette clean and packing his tools away in a wooden case. He carefully removed the wet oil painting and handed it to Bethany, who propped it up on a rock. Then he folded up the easel and, wiping his hands on his rag, turned to Fargo.

Asa Dalrimple's blue eyes were sharp over his thick white beard. They shone with humor and intelligence. But there was also suffering there, Fargo saw. Beneath his beret, the old man wore his white hair long, like those European artist types. His battered black frock coat was cut in a loose flowing style and he'd knotted a wild purple scarf around the neck of his shirt.

"Now, who might you be?" Dalrimple asked.

"The name's Skye Fargo."

There was a flicker of recognition in the old man's eyes, interest, and . . . wariness. But his face betrayed nothing. Neither did his words. "Nice to meet you, sir."

"I was just suggesting to your daughter that you get

into town for the night," Fargo said. He hesitated a moment before deciding what to say next. On one hand, he wanted to impress upon these two incompetents the fact that there were dangers out here—like two dozen armed and desperate men. On the other hand, his instinct told him not to tip his hand about what he knew and his reason for being there. Chances were the men he'd left behind in the forest would stay put for the night, but why take the chance? "You'd be more comfortable in a good hotel," he said at last.

"But Starkill's the next town and it's thirty miles up the road," Bethany said, coming up to them. "Why, we wouldn't get there till tomorrow morning."

"You're practically on top of it. Starkill's two miles over that next hill," Fargo said, trying to keep from rolling his eyes. Asa and Bethany looked at each other in surprise and delight. The two tenderhorns didn't even know where the hell they were. "Come on, I'll help you get packed and take you there."

Half an hour later, just as the last of the light was leaving the western sky, they rode into Starkill. It wasn't much of a town. Here and there, oil lamps hanging from the eaves of the stores lit the scene dimly. Beyond the false-fronted stores lining the dusty main street were some sod houses and a couple of tents pitched on the back streets. There wasn't even much of a saloon, just a small open-fronted store with a sign that read DRINKING. Another joint was called THE EATERY, and inside the window, Fargo could see people gathered around rude tables. Starkill was a hardscrabble community on the edge of wilderness and there weren't many folks out on the streets.

The few folks he saw in passing wagons and on the boardwalks wore simple clothes of homespun and sheepskin. From what he observed, Fargo knew immediately that most of the locals were ranchers. He'd seen scores of towns like this one and he knew the kind of life ranchers led. To carve out your own ranch meant battling the blasting heat of summer when your cattle went thirsty and their black tongues hung out of their mouths, and fighting the winter ice storms when your herd froze like statues. It was a damn hard life. Only the toughest survived. It was clear that nobody around Starkill was making much of a living, if you counted it in money. But they were making a good life. Over and over again, he saw the few men and women greeting one another and stopping to talk and pass on gossip. It seemed like a friendly and close-knit community.

As they rode through, nearly everybody they passed stopped to stare openly at the three of them, less at Fargo's tall frame atop his black-and-white pinto than at Asa Dalrimple in his beret and purple scarf, his easel strapped to the side of his horse. And most especially, the men stared at Bethany and her extravagant red hair and cherry-colored frock.

At the end of the street, Fargo spotted a sign that read HOTEL. They dismounted and tethered the horses. Inside, an ample grandmotherly-looking woman with a knot of gray hair introduced herself as Mrs. Murphy. She had them sign the guest register and then prepared to lead them up the narrow stairs to show them their rooms.

"I'm going to stable the horses first," Fargo said, pocketing his room key. He was eager to get on with business. There was no time to lose.

"Oh," Bethany said, turning about on the stairway while her father and Mrs. Murphy continued on up. Bethany wasn't trying to hide the disappointment in her blue eyes. "But . . . I thought . . . maybe you'd join us for dinner, Mr. Fargo." Her fingers played with the top button of her high-necked dress. "After all, I—my pa and I—owe you thanks for getting us into town."

Fargo smiled, wondering just how grateful she'd be. She was hard to read, seeming so innocent yet with that mysterious quality he couldn't quite put his finger on.

"Well, if you're over at the Eatery later, I'll look in on you," he said. "Or I'll see you around tomorrow."

"Are you going to be in town long?" Bethany asked. She stepped down one step and came up close to him.

Fargo reached out one arm and wrapped it around her waist, drawing her close. She came willingly, pliant as a green willow, as he bent to kiss her lightly, just brushing his lips against hers, inhaling the warm perfume of her that rose from her neck, her thick hair. Then he let her go. She blushed uncertainly and held on to the railing.

"Yeah, I'll be around a few days at least," he said lightly. He touched the brim of his hat and stepped out into the night. Horses first. He led their three mounts to a stable he'd spotted just off the main street. An inspection of the stalls and the oat bins satisfied him that the Ovaro would be well taken care of. Then he walked to the main street and retraced his steps to a storefront he'd passed on the way in. The sign read STARKILL SHERIFF. The windows were dark. Fargo knocked anyway. No sound inside. He looked around. A group of passing ranchmen paused when they spotted him and Fargo nodded a greeting.

"I'm looking for the sheriff," he said. "Anybody know where he's at?"

"Sure, stranger," one of the men said. "At this hour, you can always find him having dinner over there." He jerked his thumb toward the Eatery.

Fargo crossed the street and walked into the crowded room. Rustic wooden tables and chairs took up most of the space. At one end of the room was a giant stone fireplace where gobbets of meat were sizzling on spits and a row of pots steamed the spicy odor of bean chili. A rotund bald man with a big smile and half his teeth missing hurried by with a tray of grilled steaks. Fargo figured he was the proprietor and signaled to him on his way back to the kitchen.

"I'm Eddie Bly, proprietor of this here establishment," the bald man said in a booming voice as he paused to wipe his hands on his white apron. "Can I get you some grub, stranger?"

"I'm looking for the sheriff," Fargo shouted over the hubbub.

"Sheriff? he's here every night," the rotund man shouted back with a gap-toothed smile. "Sits right over . . ." He started to point to a small table in the corner, but it was empty. The man scanned the room once, then twice, a puzzled look on his face. He glanced at the large clock on the wall, then scratched his head. "That's strange," he said in a low voice that Fargo almost didn't catch above the noise. "That's strange—" he said again, louder for Fargo's benefit. "Sheriff Doug Simpkinson ain't never missed dinner here in four years." The proprietor was called by one of his customers, and as he moved away, he again glanced over his shoulder to the empty spot where the sheriff usually sat.

Fargo walked out of the Eatery into the cool night air. For the next half hour he checked the drinking establishment and every store, careful to give some innocuous excuse for wanting to find the sheriff so as not to cause alarm or get tongues wagging. But Sheriff Doug Simpkinson was nowhere to be found. At least nowhere in Starkill.

As Fargo stood on the boardwalk in front of the Sheriff's office, gazing down the quiet streets of the town of Starkill, he thought of the men in the forest. There was big trouble coming to this little town. Like an echo, he heard the men's raucous laughter and the one man's voice that had cried out in defiance, in anger, in fear. Then the three gunshots. Yeah. Could be. It could be that it had been Sheriff Doug Simpkinson in the forest that afternoon, murdered by those men.

Fargo swore silently. If Simpkinson had been killed, then he was now in this all alone. He felt the weight of the secret he'd sworn not to tell. And now he was one man against a couple dozen. Yeah, big trouble was heading to the town of Starkill.

2

Yeah, the town of Starkill looked peaceful, Fargo thought as he watched a few of its citizens hurrying along the boardwalk through the cold spring night air. From down the street came an occasional burst of laughter or a shout from the small storefront that promised DRINKING. But it was the quietest saloon in the West, he thought. And the one chow joint in town, the Eatery, had even less ruckus. Starkill was peaceful all right, but it sure wasn't going to stay that way.

Fargo spotted two familiar figures emerging from the front door of the hotel. Bethany and her father were heading out to get some supper. He walked across the dusty street cut deep with the ruts of wagon wheels to join them.

"Fargo!" Bethany called out. "Care to join us?" She'd changed her clothes and was wearing an emerald-green striped dress that hugged every curve of her and plunged low in the neckline lined with lace. She'd pinned up her hair to show off her long pale neck and a green feather nestled among her auburn curls. Dalrimple had tied a bright red scarf around his neck and was carrying a big black portfolio under one arm. He nodded a greeting to Fargo and repeated his daughter's invitation.

Fargo gave Bethany his arm and the three of them

swept along the boardwalk toward the gold-lit windows of the Eatery. Every man they passed stopped to watch Bethany. Inside, they made their way to a corner table. The place had calmed down a little, but heads turned when they walked in. A skinny man with bushy muttonchops was tuning his fiddle in the corner, and when he spotted Bethany, he winked at her and started playing "Sweet Rosie O'Grady." The rotund proprietor, Eddie Bly, came along in a moment to take their orders and returned a few minutes later with thick steaks, fried tomatoes, and mugs of beer. Fargo ate with gusto, enjoying every bite. The food was simple but good.

"You're a damn good painter," Fargo said after a while to Dalrimple. "You specialize in painting landscapes?"

"Oh, Pa can do anything! Anything at all!" Bethany said enthusiastically, then stopped. Fargo saw her blush as she and her father exchanged glances.

"I do portraiture, too," the old man said, clearing his throat. "But I am always looking for unusual scenery, for places no one has ever painted before. If I could just find a place like that, the paintings I could do might make me nationally famous. Tell me, Mr. Fargo, in all your wanderings in the West, what's the strangest and most interesting landscape you've seen?"

"There's a place north of here that's pretty spectacular," Fargo said after a moment's thought. "It's called Colter's Hell. There are pits of boiling mud, lakes that steam like soup, and geysers that shoot up into the sky—"

Fargo paused when he observed their faces. The change was instantaneous. Bethany Dalrimple went white as a sheet and the old man looked as frightened as if he might be suffering a heart attack.

"Why—why are you—why do you think I would want to paint this—this place called Colter's Hell?" Dalrimple sputtered.

Fargo wondered what the hell was going on. "Well, nobody's ever painted it before," he said, watching them carefully but pretending not to notice their distress. "Lots of people think the first white man to see it, John Colter, was flat out lying about it. But I went through there once. And it's strange land all right. Just like he said."

"You've . . . you've been there?" Bethany squeaked.

"Yeah," Fargo said. "Got chased through it once by a swarm of angry Blackfeet. But I'm not sure I'd recommend you ride up and start drawing pictures of Colter's Hell. It's Shoshoni territory now and they don't always welcome white visitors."

"Right," Dalrimple said. He tugged at the silk scarf at his throat as if it had suddenly gotten too tight.

"So, why are you two so squeamish about Colter's Hell?" Fargo asked them. The question obviously took them aback. Asa Dalrimple gaped like a fish and Bethany twisted her handkerchief. She recovered first.

"Squeamish?" she said with a nervous laugh. "I have no idea what you're talking about, Skye. Why, I've never even heard of this place before."

Fargo let it drop. There was some secret here. Something to do with Colter's Hell that Bethany and Dalrimple didn't want to discuss. Fargo wondered what it could be. Then his thoughts turned darker as he remembered the men in the forest and the trouble that was about to descend on Starkill. They ate their servings of hot apple pie and coffee in silence, listening to the fiddler sawing away in the corner.

When the plates were cleared away, Dalrimple leaned down and retrieved his big black portfolio. He unfastened it and removed a large pad of paper and a paper packet of colored chalks. Fargo was amused to see Bethany stand and fluff up her hair, then seat herself on the table in a striking pose, her head thrown back. The old man positioned his chair with his back to the room and began to sketch her with the chalks, using bold exaggerated gestures. They had obviously done this before and the act was very effective.

In moments most of the patrons had gathered around to watch. Even the fiddler stopped playing and approached. Fargo leaned over after a few minutes and saw that Asa Dalrimple had drawn an instant portrait of his daughter, accurately capturing the proud tilt of her head, the soft waves of her thick hair, the extravagant curve of her white throat, and even a hint of the shadowy fullness of her cleavage.

"Voilà! C'est fini!" Asa Dalrimple announced grandly. "That's how we artistes say it's finished," he explained to the crowd. He held up the portrait and several of the men applauded. "Four dollars a picture," Dalrimple said. Fargo could see the women tugging on their husbands' sleeves and whispered conversations taking place. Bethany slid down off the table and Fargo pulled her toward him, away from the crowd.

"Your pa's busy now. Care to dance?" he asked her, slipping his arm around her narrow waist. Bethany looked up at him and giggled, her pale blue eyes merry.

But once again, Fargo was struck by the idea that she was carrying some kind of sorrow, that she was a woman who didn't have a chance to be happy very often. He flipped a silver dollar to the fiddler, who started off with "Turkey in the Straw." Fargo asked him for something slower.

Bethany pressed her warm curves against him. She wasn't shy, he thought as he stroked her back and enjoyed the sensation of her pillowy breasts against his broad hard chest, her thigh brushing his. He inhaled her perfume, the natural odor of her skin like violets, then nuzzled her neck and felt her shiver under his touch. They danced for an hour until Fargo felt that Bethany had melted into his body, until he had come to know her curves under his hands, the way she moved against him. Her fragrant nearness aroused him, he felt himself harden, swelling against the tight Levi's. She felt it, too, as he held her near, and she blushed at first, then gazed into his eyes.

"Let's go back to the hotel," he whispered in her ear. She nodded and he guided her through the edge of the crowd that was still gathered around Asa Dalrimple, everyone watching transfixed as Dalrimple sketched a pair of ranch hands posing awkwardly on two chairs.

"Your father's damn good," Fargo said to Bethany as they walked up the boardwalk, his arm around her. "Seems like a man who can paint like that ought to get real famous."

Bethany didn't answer, and when Fargo glanced at her, he saw that she had tears in her eyes. She brushed them away quickly and he didn't ask what it was all about. Women told you what was going on in their own sweet time. And there was no way to rush them. About anything.

They climbed the stairs, and when they reached Bethany's door, she unlocked it, then turned toward him. Her cheeks were pink, her eyes bright, and the swelling mounds of her breasts moved with her quickened breath. He could see that the hour of dancing together had aroused her as much as it had him.

"Maybe . . . maybe it's too soon," she whispered. "I think I should say good night now."

"Up to you," Fargo said, keeping the disappointment from his voice. Never rush a woman, he reminded himself. "Good night, then."

He started to step back, but she put her hand on his arm and pulled at him, then came into his arms. He bent to kiss her, only this time he didn't just brush her lips. She opened to him as his tongue slid into her sweet mouth and she seemed to dissolve against him. She moaned softly, deep in her throat, like a kitten purring. He was hard now, straining to be inside her, hot and pulsing. He pulled away and she seemed breathless.

"Yes, yes," she breathed. "Tonight, Skye. Now."

He bent down and picked her up in his powerful arms, surprised at the lightness of her. He pushed open the door and closed it behind him with his heel, then crossed the dark room to the big brass bed. He laid her down, outstretched on the bed, her green silk dress rustling around her. Then he kissed her again, his tongue exploring her mouth deeply as she sucked on him, hungrily. Her heart was beating as fast as a bird's. He could feel her hand desperately unbuttoning her bodice, then heard her breath gasping. She fumbled at the buttons of his shirt, hurrying. Fargo pulled away and stood by the bed.

"Is . . . is something the matter?" Bethany asked him. He could barely see her expression in the dark room.

"Nope," Fargo answered. "I just like to see what I'm doing." He pulled the tinderbox from his shirt pocket and struck it, then lit the oil lamp by the bed, trimming the wick. A golden glow lit the room, throwing dancing shadows into the corners. Bethany sat up on the bed, looking worried. Fargo sat down beside her and gently began undoing her bodice, one button at a time, and her dress opened to reveal the white lace camisole beneath, the high roundness of her smooth breasts.

"Let's take this slowly," Fargo said, stripping off his shirt and his boots. "I want to enjoy every minute of it."

He slipped his hand beneath the lace to cup her warm full breast like ripe fruit that suddenly spilled over the top of her camisole. The pale pink nipples were crinkled with pleasure and he bent to tongue first one and then the other, licking the circles of her tender areolae, flicking across the delicate points until she cried out with pleasure, her fingers wound in his hair. She stroked his broad chest and the rippling muscles of his biceps, lightly, teasingly. He was throbbing, aching to be inside her. But in no hurry.

He felt her touch him, tentatively, shyly, stroking the hard bulge beneath his Levi's. He slipped her out of her dress, then her camisole and bloomers, until she lay on the bed in her lace garters and white stockings. The golden flickering light glinted on the dark auburn triangle between her thighs and he slipped his finger up into her slick tight warmth, probing, rubbing her as she began moving under him like a bucking horse, bringing her close to the edge. Her sweet musk filled the room.

Bethany moaned, tossing her long hair from side to side.

"Oh, Skye. Yes, there. There. Oh, oh, God!"

He stopped suddenly, stripped off his Levi's and shorts. His huge cock was rock hard, throbbing. Her eyes widened. He pushed her knees apart and she guided him inside as he pushed, slowly. Her hot tunnel widened to take his hard rod inside her.

"Oh, oh, Skye. Yes, how I wanted you inside me—oh!"

He began moving, in and out, stroking her, pushing deep inside her, stretching her. Her legs came open and she took him in deeper. He cupped his hands around her small tight ass and lifted her up against him as he plunged in, again and again, his rod rigid with explosive force. Her warm satiny sheath felt like it was made for him. As he plunged into her, he stroked her, felt her nearing the edge again, her breathing fast. He cupped her breasts, squeezed the nipples gently, and she cried out, inarticulately, and he felt her contract, her body shuddering with the climax as he felt his balls on fire, the hot urgency of gushing, the explosion of lava shooting out of him, pumping up into her again and again.

"Oh God! Yes, yes, oh, stop! Stop!" she cried out as he plunged into her, felt her racked by pleasure as he shot into her. Finally he slowed, stroked more slowly, then stopped. He kissed her lips lightly, then her eyelids. Her eyes fluttered open.

"Oh, Skye," she murmured. "That was incredible. I've . . . I've never come like that before. Ever. Thank you."

"No thanks necessary," he said, kissing her again. "I consider that a pretty fair exchange."

Bethany laughed and tried to tickle him, but he got her instead. Then he lay beside her and she cuddled next to him under the quilt. After a few minutes she was asleep, breathing gently. Fargo leaned over and blew out the oil lamp, then lay back on the big brass bed.

The dim light from the street washed across the ceiling of the small hotel room. His thoughts went back to the forest and the wary gang of men, the three gunshots. He hoped to hell they hadn't ambushed Sheriff Doug Simpkinson. But he knew that was exactly what had happened. And now his thoughts turned to what they would do next. Now that he had caught up to them, he found himself facing them down alone. And he wondered what they'd do next. Sleep was a long time coming.

Bethany rolled over sleepily just as he was pulling on his boots. She sat up, her tangled auburn hair wild around her face and gleaming in the morning sun that poured through the windows.

"You're leaving so soon?" She stretched her arms and Fargo enjoyed the view of her full pink-tipped breasts before she pulled the quilt up to her chin. As he grabbed his hat, he bent over the bed and kissed her.

"It's already nine o'clock, sleepyhead," he said. "And I've got business to take care of." Yeah, like finding out where the hell Sheriff Doug Simpkinson was. She clung to him for a moment.

"After breakfast, I'm going to take a nice hot bath,"

Bethany said. She played with his ear. "Wouldn't you like to join me?"

"Sure would," Fargo said. "But not this morning."

"But when . . . when will . . . I see you again?" she asked, sounding suddenly insecure.

"As soon as possible," he reassured her. "I'll look in on you later today." He let himself out her door and went down the hall to his own room. Mrs. Murphy had put his leather grip on the bed. The pitcher on the washstand was full of water. He splashed it over his face and neck, changed into clean clothes, and headed first for the stable to check on his horse. The black-and-white pinto was glad to see him, kicking at the wooden stall and whinnying.

"A fine critter," the stablekeeper said, pouring more oats into the feeding trough. Fargo looked around to make sure the straw was fresh and there was room for the pinto to exercise in the yard. He made sure the Ovaro had enough water and that it would receive a good long curry. While he was there, he decided he'd check on Dalrimple's nags, but he saw only one of them.

"Have I seen the old man with the beret?" the stablekeeper repeated Fargo's question. "Oh sure, he came by here at dawn loaded down with some big black case and a wooden box like a suitcase. Said he was heading out to paint pictures of the wild mountains. Said he'd be back for sure later today, though."

For a moment Fargo considered taking the Ovaro and heading out in pursuit of Dalrimple. He didn't like the idea of the old man wandering around outside the Starkill town limits with that gang of men on the loose. On the other hand, Dalrimple had left several hours before. It would be impossible to guess which direction he'd gone or track him on the well-traveled roads that led out of town.

He was distracted from his thoughts by the sound of shouting and pounding hoofbeats. Fargo left the stable and found the main street of Starkill in a state of chaos. People were running every which way and women were screaming in terror. Men were loading their rifles, shouting in confusion. Ed Bly was ringing the bell that hung outside the Eatery and the clanging resounded through the air.

"Federal marshal's coming! Federal marshal's heading into town!" the man was calling out.

A line of riders came sweeping by, galloping in a long line down the main street. Fargo saw the trail-hardened faces, the flint-sharp eyes, their holsters and saddle scabbards packed with gleaming firearms. At the end of the street, he could see that a line of men had fanned out, barring the way so that no one could get in or out of town. Federal marshal, bullshit! It was them all right. The gang of men he'd trailed for two months. They seemed to be taking over the whole town of Starkill.

For a moment he cursed himself silently. He should have organized the men of Starkill against just such an invasion. But then he realized he couldn't have. He'd sworn to keep the secret of why he was hunting these men. And if he couldn't explain why they were dangerous, it would have been impossible to get the Starkill men mobilized.

He pushed his way into the crowd. Everyone was muttering and excited. Then he spotted a heavy mountain wagon rolling down the street. Riding in advance of it on a gleaming white stallion was a stocky man with black greased-back hair that shone in the sun like black fire. His leather jacket looked new, as did his silver-chased saddle. The man's eyes, sunk deep in his thick face, scanned the town as if he could see through everything.

Fargo stepped back behind a wagon and watched the man pass by, followed by the lumbering wagon covered up by a sheet of canvas. When it reached the center of town, the procession halted. Fargo spotted Bethany as she emerged onto the porch of the hotel, wearing a straw sun hat and a yellow dress. She looked around in surprise at all the people crowded into the street. Even from a distance she was stunningly beautiful, Fargo thought as he envisioned her on the brass bed. He wrested the pleasant picture from his mind.

The stocky man stood up in his stirrups. The big white stallion shifted under him, but he didn't lose his balance. He was an impressive figure, obviously used to leadership. The citizens of Starkill were crowded on the boardwalks and hanging out of the windows to see him. Ed Bly stopped ringing the bell and there was a silence, broken only by the creak of the leather saddles. Fargo scanned the rows of men on their horses. So this is what they looked like up close. Yeah, they were tough. Every damned one of them. Fargo decided to stay out of sight until he could figure out what to do next.

"I'm Federal Marshal James Tritt," the stocky man suddenly called out.

Federal marshal, sure, Fargo said to himself. James Tritt was lying, but the townspeople seemed impressed, muttering to each other.

"You folks got a mayor here?" Tritt shouted.

"No, sir!" Ed Bly called out, stepping forward from the crowd on the front stoop of his chow joint. "We got no need of a mayor. But we got a sheriff. Sheriff Doug Simpkinson."

Tritt leaned forward in his saddle and suddenly pulled the canvas off the mountain wagon. There, as Fargo feared, lay the body of Doug Simpkinson. His chest was marked by the dark holes of two bullets and his temple by a third. Simpkinson's eyes were still open, his gaze fixed toward the clear blue sky. Several women screamed at the sight and a hubbub of anger rose from the crowd.

"You're wondering who killed your sheriff," James Tritt shouted over the noise, which ceased at once. His voice was resonant, compelling. "Well, I'll tell you. There's an armed and dangerous man in this territory. This posse has been tracking him for two months now. He's been on a killing spree all across the territory. Women and children, all slaughtered. He killed your sheriff. You could be next."

Tritt paused for effect. The citizens of Starkill talked excitedly.

It was time to stir up some trouble, sow some seeds of doubt, Fargo decided. "How come we didn't read about it in the Cheyenne newspaper?" he called out in a loud voice. He ducked back behind the wagon so he wouldn't be spotted by Tritt and his men.

"Yeah!" another man said. "Yeah, he's right!" Others took up the cry.

"Hey wait a minute!" It was Ed Bly shouting. "You tell us, Mr. Federal Marshal, how come we ain't heard

43

about this? If there's been trouble nearby, we'd hear about it. That time those bank robbers over in—"

"The government," James Tritt cut in smoothly. "The government doesn't want this bastard to know we're onto him. Those are my orders."

James Tritt had nothing to do with being a federal marshal. The whole thing was a lie from beginning to end, Fargo thought. He'd met a lot of marshals riding through the Western territories, and if there was one thing they did, it was to pass on information, to let folks know when there was trouble around so they could be ready for it. The whole idea of keeping this kind of a secret was ridiculous.

"You're lying!" Fargo shouted again, and then ducked out of sight. The crowd started babbling and Fargo could tell that Tritt's men were looking around trying to locate the troublemaker.

"Yeah, just hold on," Bly took up the protest. "Last time that marshal—" But James Tritt started talking again and some of the townspeople shushed up Ed Bly.

"This murder speaks for itself," Tritt continued, gesturing at Doug Simpkinson's bloody corpse. "We know he's around here, probably hiding out right in your town. My men will be patrolling this whole area until we find him. We expect your full cooperation. This man is armed and dangerous. He's one of the Goddard Gang."

Fargo felt a wave of surprise hit him. The Goddard Gang. At the name of the criminals, notorious two decades earlier, people began talking again. Fargo overheard a woman saying, "I thought they put those men in jail years ago." But then his attention was attracted by a sudden movement on the porch of the hotel.

He glanced that way and saw Bethany take a staggering step and clutch the railing. A man standing beside her offered his arm. She looked distraught; in fact she looked terrified.

"So, for the time being," James Tritt was saying, "I'm taking over here as acting sheriff of Starkill." He leaned over and removed the shiny tin star from Doug Simpkinson's vest and pinned it on his own leather jacket.

Fargo had decided this charade had gone on long enough. It was time for action. He pulled the Colt from his holster and started to step forward out of the crowd. "And now that I'm sheriff," Tritt continued, "I want every—"

"If anybody's going to be sheriff, it's going to be me," a deep voice cut in. The townspeople craned their necks to see who had interrupted, and Fargo felt a wave of shock and then relief as he recognized the figure riding forward through the crowd.

"Mike Ford," Fargo muttered to himself. "I'll be damned." Mike Ford was one of the U.S. Treasury's best agents, often working undercover. Fargo had run into him once before and had a lot of respect for the lawman, for his ice-cool head and his sure aim. Ford was a blond man, his hair like a golden helmet in the sun, his face tanned and etched with hard planes, his brown eyes piercing and his shoulders broad. Hell, Fargo thought. Things had gotten pretty serious if they were sending Mike Ford in to Starkill to help him out.

Fargo held the Colt in his hand, ready for action. James Tritt had turned angrily in his saddle to see who had dared interfere. The moment was silent, tension in the air.

"That's right," Mike Ford continued. "I've got a paper here from the governor of Wyoming Territory dated a week ago. I've been officially appointed deputy to Sheriff Douglas Simpkinson." Ford waved a piece of paper in front of him. "And since Sheriff Simpkinson is dead, I take his place. That makes me sheriff."

James Tritt held out his hand for the paper, but Mike Ford leaned over and passed it to Ed Bly, who was standing nearby on the porch. Tritt gritted his teeth. Everyone in the crowd seemed to hold their breath as Bly scrutinized the paper and then looked up.

"Yeah, looks right as rain," Bly announced. "It's all legal like I guess we got Sheriff Mike Ford here in Starkill." Fargo knew he wasn't imagining the slight note of relief in Ed Bly's voice. Clearly Bly sensed something wasn't right about Federal Marshal James Tritt and his posse and was relieved not to have him suddenly running the town, lock, stock, and barrel.

"Well," Tritt said coldly, trying hard to keep the irritation from his voice, "welcome to Starkill, Sheriff Mike Ford. My men and I can use all the help we can get. Now, the first thing we got to do is—"

"*I'll* decide what Starkill's going to do," Mike Ford said. "And the first thing is that any man who's not a citizen of Starkill will turn in his weapon right now at the sheriff's office. This is a law-abiding town and I won't have a bunch of strangers riding through with firearms. Federal marshal or not. So, if you plan to stay in town, I expect you in my office to check in your weapons."

Tritt swore a curse and Fargo grinned. Mike Ford sure knew how to play a damned good game. But it was a dangerous game, Fargo knew. Mike Ford swung down off his horse, retrieved his rifle from the saddle scabbard, and mounted the steps to the sheriff's office. Fargo stepped out from behind the wagon and pushed his way through the crowd. Mike Ford was just unlocking the door to the sheriff's office when Fargo came up beside him.

"Sheriff Ford?" Fargo touched the brim of his hat. "I'd like to have a word with you."

Mike Ford glanced up and started when he recognized Fargo. For a brief instant a grin lit up his tanned face, but he quickly sobered. "Don't think we've met, stranger," Ford said in a loud voice, obviously for the benefit of bystanders. "But come on inside."

Mike Ford was a cool customer, Fargo thought, keeping his own expression as stony-faced as a cautious poker player with a full house. Ford got the door open and they walked inside. Behind them, Fargo heard Tritt giving his men the orders to dismount.

The sheriff's office was pretty bare. Simpkinson's wooden chair and rolltop desk stood beside the door. Tacked to the walls were maps of the territory and a couple of wanted posters. A rifle rack held a row of firearms. A few chairs were scattered around and the back wall of the room was taken up by the bars of the jail cell that held a cot and a bucket.

Fargo knew they had just moments alone together before Tritt or some of the men of Starkill would follow them inside. "Real surprise to see you here," he said to Mike Ford. "This thing must have gotten a whole lot more serious if they sent you in."

"Yeah. It's gotten real serious," Mike Ford said. There was little time to talk. Outside, James Tritt was shouting directions to his men. He'd follow them at any moment. "Glad it wasn't you in the wagon under that canvas," he added. "I thought it might be. Sheriff Doug Simpkinson was a good man. Bad loss for the town."

Fargo quickly filled Ford in on what he'd witnessed the day before in the forest and how he'd been following the gang at the request of Doug Simpkinson for two months.

"So you know what this is all about," Mike Ford said.

"Only some of it," Fargo said. "When I was hired for this job, they told me it's about money, counterfeit bills."

"Best counterfeit bills ever made," Mike said. "Best fakes the U.S. Treasury has ever seen. You understand, if word of this got out—"

"Sure," Fargo said. "They told me it's gotta be kept secret or there'd be a panic in every bank in the West."

"That's right," Mike confirmed. "If folks didn't trust the U.S. currency, there'd be chaos and every bank and store would go belly-up, decent law-abiding folks would lose their savings. It would be a disaster."

"Now, I've been following Jim Tritt and his gang through three territories for the past two months now," Fargo added. "What I don't understand is what Tritt is up to." He heard footsteps crossing the wooden porch outside. There was no time for more conversation.

"I'll fill you in later on the rest," Mike said hastily. "We're not sure either exactly what Tritt's got up his sleeve, but we know he's connected to this counterfeit scheme. And I'll have to check on this Goddard Gang connection. That doesn't make sense to me. So, if you get a chance," he added, "throw your lot in with Tritt.

Find out what he's after. Keep your eyes open and back against the wall."

Fargo moved away from Mike Ford a moment be the two men walked through the door. James Tritt was followed by a bruiser close to seven feet tall, with arms like trees and brown hair that hung in greasy shanks to his shoulders. He seemed to be Tritt's right-hand man.

James Tritt crossed the bare wooden floor, sat down in the sheriff's chair, and put his boots up on the desk. Ford ignored him and shot Fargo a glance, then crossed to the rack, where he put up his rifle.

"This is my assistant marshal, Bruno Riker," Tritt said laconically. Huge and greasy, Riker stood just inside the door idly swinging his fists, his small eyes shifting from one face to the other. Bruno Riker was one of the ugliest and biggest men Fargo had ever seen. Riker locked eyes with him for a moment, then looked back to Mike Ford. Riker didn't look too smart, his eyes holding an expression that was blank, yet deadly.

"Now, I got all my men surrounding Starkill," Tritt boasted. "You'll thank me for it later, Ford. I've got this town locked up tight. Nobody can escape. This afternoon, we'll do a house-to-house search."

"Aren't you jumping the gun, Tritt?" Mike Ford asked coolly. He took down one of Sheriff Simpkinson's rifles and buffed the barrel with a chamois cloth.

"Yeah, just why are you so sure this desperado is here in Starkill?" Fargo cut in. "He could be halfway to Denver City by now."

"And who the hell are you?" Tritt snarled, seeming to notice him for the first time.

"The name's Skye Fargo."

At his name, James Tritt set his jaw and exchanged looks with the big man standing in the corner. It was clear they knew his reputation.

"I've heard about you," Tritt said under his breath.

"Well, well. The famous Trailsman." Ford was obviously trying to sound surprised. "You've got a damn good reputation. We can probably use some help from you. Tracking down this murderer."

"Sure," Tritt said smoothly. "Sure, we could use some help from the famous Trailsman. We need all the help we can get."

"And, I'm repeating my question, Tritt. Just why do you think this murderer is hiding out in Starkill?" Fargo asked.

"I *know* he's here!" Tritt shouted as he brought his fist down on the desk impatiently. "Listen, you two. I've been a lawman for thirty years and I know the criminal mind. You let me search this town and I'll collar that bastard. He's here all right. I can smell him. Like I said, the first thing to do is a house-to-house search."

"You haven't told us anything about him," Fargo pointed out. "Except that he was in the Goddard Gang. I thought those guys were locked up in jail a long time ago."

"Yeah, they were in prison, but this one's out now," Tritt growled impatiently.

"So, what's his name? You know what he looks like?" Fargo shot back.

"Hell, the bastard's got a hundred aliases," Tritt snapped. "But yeah, I know what he looks like. Soon as I lay eyes on him, the whole jig's up! And while we're sitting here wasting time, that bastard's probably getting away from us. Hell, Sheriff, I just want to do my job."

Mike Ford moved calmly and smoothly. He pulled up the rifle and held it across his chest. He didn't aim it, but the threat was there. "My job is to restore law and order to this town," he said. "And to get everybody calmed down. What I said goes, Tritt. This town's under my jurisdiction. Now, either you and your men check in your firearms with me right now. Or else you get out of town. That goes for you, too, Fargo. What's it going to be?"

Tritt rose to his feet, his face flushed with anger.

"Sure, Ford," Tritt said, his voice shaking with rage. "If that's the way you want it. Sure, we'll get out of your town. But that Goddard Gang member is somewhere here in Starkill. And I'll be right outside town waiting for him. Sounds like you're not even interested in catching the bastard."

Fargo realized it was time to throw his lot in with Tritt, to win his trust. If he was going to find out what the man was up to, he mustn't seem too cozy with the new sheriff.

"Sounds to me like that, too," Fargo lied. Tritt shot him a surprised glance, then smirked. "Sounds to me like the new sheriff might have a touch of yellow on his belly. I say we ride out and find this crook, then string him up high."

Mike Ford narrowed his eyes and gripped the rifle tighter. It was a good act they were putting on. And Jim Tritt bought it.

"Why don't you come join up with me, Fargo?" Tritt asked with a laugh. "We're looking for some real men to help us out. We're going to scour this countryside for this Goddard bastard and keep this town under lock and key until that man walks into our net."

"Sounds good to me," Fargo said.

"Then get out of here," Mike Ford said. "All three of you. Get out of my town."

"Sure, you yellow belly," Jim Tritt said with a laugh. After a moment the big Bruno Riker laughed, too. It was possible that the huge man was hard of hearing since he had only laughed when he saw Tritt laughing. The two of them turned to go. Fargo gave Mike Ford a grin as he left the office.

Outside, the citizens of Starkill were still milling in the street, huddling in small groups and looking anxiously toward the sheriff's office. As he crossed the wooden porch, Fargo heard the click of a rifle catch behind him.

"Hey, Tritt," Mike Ford's voice called out.

Fargo turned around, as did Tritt, to see the sheriff standing in the doorway, his rifle aimed straight at Tritt. Riker had apparently not heard anything and continued on.

"Aren't you forgetting something?" Ford asked. He leveled the rifle again at Tritt's chest, where Doug Simpkinson's tin star was gleaming in the sun.

"Oh, sure," Tritt said with exaggerated politeness. He ripped the star off his chest and tossed it at Mike Ford's feet. "Take your star, Mr. Sheriff. Just don't count on a piece of tin to stop a bullet if that Goddard Gang bastard gets near you." He laughed and mounted his horse.

"I'll meet you at the edge of town," Fargo said. Just before turning toward the stables, he glanced over his shoulder and saw Ford still standing in the doorway,

pinning the tin star on his chest. Fargo gave him a subtle thumbs-up sign. Yeah, their plan was working. For
the moment.

A few minutes later he was riding on the Ovaro on
the road that led out of town. Just beyond the last of the
wooden buildings, a line of men stood ranged across the
dusty street, rifles at the ready. Fargo glanced in both
directions and saw that Tritt had posted one of his men
every few hundred feet all the way around the town.
Yeah, it would be impossible for anybody to come or go
without being seen by one of his men. Tritt and the rest
of his gang, about a dozen men, were on horseback,
waiting a hundred feet up the road. Who the hell were
they looking for? What were they up to?

"All right," Tritt shouted as he saw Fargo riding toward them. "We're going to ride out and find this bastard. And we got the famous Trailsman to help us do it."

"Right," Fargo said. "First thing is, you take me to the
spot you found Doug Simpkinson's body. I'll pick up the
trail from there."

There was an uneasy silence broken only by the jangle
of spurs and the creak of leather as Tritt's men exchanged uneasy glances. Fargo pretended not to notice
their discomfort. They sure as hell didn't want to take
him to the spot where they had murdered Simpkinson
the day before.

"Good plan," Tritt said smoothly after a moment.
"Let's ride."

The mounted men moved forward and Fargo found
himself suddenly surrounded on all sides by the tough
trail-hardened followers of Jim Tritt, men who had cold-
bloodedly murdered Doug Simpkinson just the day be-

fore, scar-faced hard-hearted men with death in their eyes.

They rode hard for three hours, circling through the back country, galloping through grassy meadows tinged with the early-spring green, and through deep pine forests where traces of snow still lingered. By late afternoon Fargo knew Jim Tritt was leading them farther and farther away from the spot where they'd murdered Simpkinson.

They came to a rocky outcropping and a slope of tumbled boulders where a stream babbled at the foot of towering rocks through a stand of young pine trees. The sky was golden with the coming sunset. Tritt called a halt to let the horses have some water and all the men dismounted.

Fargo hesitated, remaining on the Ovaro. "I'll scout up ahead a little and circle back," he announced.

Tritt's face darkened. "Riker, go with him," he ordered.

"Huh?" the big man said.

Tritt repeated his order in a louder voice.

The big man mounted his muscular bay and Fargo headed off, letting the Ovaro climb up the slightly winding trail that led up and over the rocky slope. In another hour it would be growing dark and they'd have to turn back to town. He and Riker had gone a short distance up the hill when Fargo's keen ears caught the sound of men's voices. He paused beside a huge tower of broken rock and looked around, gazing out over the folded hills, brushed with the slanting light from the lowering sun, and the young pine forest below. He heard the men's voices again. Riker apparently couldn't hear the sound and Fargo realized that the words of Tritt and his men, standing far below, were being echoed and amplified by the rocks. He listened hard and could make out the phrases.

"—get rid of him . . . and fast."

"—troublemaker."

"—surround him."

"—can blame it . . . stir up even more fear."

That last voice was unmistakably Jim Tritt's. Fargo knew exactly what they were talking about. They planned to murder him. Right here and right now. They'd shoot him like they had shot up the Sheriff Simpkinson and then they'd carry his body back to Starkill. They'd use him to scare the town into doing what they wanted.

But Starkill and the new sheriff, Mike Ford, were miles and miles away. And Fargo was one gun against a dozen.

3

Fargo glanced over at the huge form of Bruno Riker. Down the rocky slope below him, he heard the voices of Jim Tritt and the rest of the men plotting his murder. He had to act fast. He glanced around, then pulled his Colt.

"Look, Riker!" Fargo shouted, gesturing with the barrel of his pistol. "Over there!"

The big man turned in his saddle and looked toward where Fargo was pointing, between some large boulders on the crest of the hill.

"What?" Riker said uncertainly. "I don't see nothing . . ."

"See that?" Fargo shouted again. "That man who was watching us. Just disappeared over the hill. I'll bet it's that Goddard Gang fellow."

"I . . . I don't see nothing," Riker protested, looking off at the boulders. Fargo raised his Colt in the air and fired three shots into the sky.

"Hey, Tritt!" Fargo yelled down the slope. "I spotted him! He's up here. Come on!"

Fargo took off on the Ovaro, tearing up the slope. Behind him, Riker gave chase, too. Fargo felt the spot between his shoulder blades twitch as he thought of Bruno Riker riding right behind him. It would be easy for Riker to shoot him in the back if the big man were smart enough to figure out what his boss has planned. But luckily, Riker hadn't heard Tritt's orders to the rest of his men. Riker might be a strong bastard, but he was dumber than a doorknob.

The black-and-white pinto galloped up the slope followed by the big man on his bay. Behind him, Fargo could hear the shouting and noise of Jim Tritt's men as they mounted and prepared to follow. They weren't far behind. He knew that Tritt and his men would shoot to kill now. They would gun him down at the first opportunity, if they could catch him. As Fargo galloped over the crest of the hill, he saw a wide-open grassy slope before him. Hell, if Tritt and his men caught him here, he'd be dead. At the bottom of the hill, a deep pine forest reached up the slope; he headed for the dark edge of the trees, pounding down the slope, followed by Riker.

As they entered the trees, Fargo turned about and saw the dark forms of Tritt and his men come up over the crest of the hill. They spotted the two figures disappearing into the edge of the trees and began firing. A few bullets whizzed by as they plunged into the dark forest, the horses galloping all-out. Fargo hunched down across his pinto and Riker cried out in surprise.

"Hey, Mr. Tritt!" the big man called out over his shoulder. "Stop shooting! It's me! Riker!"

Tritt and his men let loose another fusillade of bullets that thwacked through the underbrush and thudded into the tree trunks. Fargo cursed Tritt, cursed a man so heartless that he would shoot at one of his own men, risk killing one of his own, to get somebody else. Just ahead, he saw a low branch and he galloped straight for it.

"This way!" he shouted at Riker. In his confusion, the

big man followed. At the last instant Fargo ducked down, and the Ovaro sailed under the tree branch. Fargo looked back to see the tall form of Bruno Riker as he galloped toward the branch. Riker started to duck, then turned his horse aside and threw up his arms all in the same moment. The branch caught Riker hard across the neck and arms. The bay screamed and took a tumble as the big man came out of the saddle and fell to earth. Fargo turned about and galloped on, focusing his attention now on the pinto. For sheer speed and agility, there was no horse like it in the West. The Ovaro surefootedly plummeted through the trees, which flashed by in a blur. The darkness of dusk was starting to gather under the pines.

Fargo heard the sounds of confusion behind him. Tritt had obviously caught up with Bruno Riker, but some of the men were also still pursuing him. For effect, Fargo shot a few more rounds of the Colt as if he was madly pursuing someone through the forest. Then he hunched down and let the pinto gallop on, bringing it around in a half circle until he was heading eastward. By the time the stars were out, he had left Tritt and his men miles behind. They'd lost his trail. He headed straight toward Starkill. He had to get back through the perimeter of men guarding the town before Tritt returned. An hour later Fargo cantered up the road and paused at the line of men at the edge of town.

"Where's the boss?" one of them asked suspiciously, surprised to see Fargo riding alone.

"We got separated," Fargo said. "I'm sure Tritt and the rest of them will be riding in any minute." The men stepped aside and let him pass.

As Fargo rode straight down the main street of Starkill, the few people hurrying along the boardwalks stopped to look at him curiously. Clearly, everybody in the town was on edge. Fargo tethered the Ovaro in front of the sheriff's office, but Mike Ford was nowhere to be seen. Across the street, the Eatery was ablaze with light, but through the windows, he saw few people inside. When he entered, he couldn't find Ford or even the proprietor, Eddie Bly, and he left word with a waitress to tell the sheriff he was looking for him. Leaving the restaurant and heading toward the hotel, Fargo wondered if Ford had maybe left him a message there.

"Sorry, Mr. Fargo," Mrs. Murphy said as she swept the feather duster across the counter. "Nobody's called for you or left anything. But . . ." She paused and glanced at him with a twinkle in her eye. "That nice young lady is upstairs and I happen to know that she and her pa ain't gone out to supper yet. I'm sure she'd be real happy for some male company. She's looked real upset all day, what with all the goings on here in Starkill."

"Thanks for the tip," Fargo said with a grin. He climbed the steps and stood before Bethany's room. A strip of dim lamplight showed underneath the door. He knocked. There was a rustle inside, the light went out. Then silence. Fargo waited and then knocked again. She was inside, but why was she pretending not to be?

"Bethany? It's me, Fargo. I know you're there. Open up."

After a slight pause he heard her footsteps cross the floor and the lock turn. The door opened a few inches. Her pale face, surrounded by her wild auburn hair, was troubled and scared. She was wearing a buckskin riding skirt and a white shirt.

"What's the matter?" Fargo asked.

Bethany smiled a false smile. "Matter?" she said. "Why . . . well, Pa's . . . not feeling well. I'm just a little worried about him."

Fargo felt the suspicions rise in him. She was lying. What was going on? "Is he inside?" he asked. "Let me see him. Maybe we should get a doctor."

"No, no, no," Bethany said a little too hastily. "I'm sure he just needs some rest."

"That's right," Asa Dalrimple's voice said from the dark room behind her. "Thank you for your concern, Fargo. I just need some rest."

Bethany started to close the door, but Fargo blocked it with his foot. "Don't lie to me, Bethany," he said. "If you're in trouble, I can help you. But you got to tell me what's going on—"

Just then, he heard the sounds of pounding hooves and men's voices. Jim Tritt and his men were riding back into town. Fargo knew he had to get downstairs and find Mike Ford. Bethany saw his indecision.

"We'll be all right," she said with a wan smile. "Pa's just feeling poorly and all those men scared me." Fargo didn't buy the excuse, but there was no time to argue now. As he hurried down the hallway, he heard Bethany close and bolt the door. Something had the two of them worried, more worried than they ought to be. But he couldn't figure out how an old painter and his pretty daughter might be connected up with Jim Tritt and his gang.

Fargo headed out the back door of the hotel and found

himself in a small alleyway. A black cat dashed across his path into the shadows. He wasn't a superstitious man, but at the moment he needed all the luck he could get. Stealthily, he moved along the street, secreting himself in dark doorways or behind corners of buildings from time to time as groups of Tritt's men rode down the street. Now, where the hell was Mike Ford?

He'd almost made it to the sheriff's office, when he saw riders approaching. Jim Tritt was in the lead and he was riding like he was mad as a hornet. Fargo ducked down behind a row of barrels and watched as Tritt and his men dismounted and ran up to the sheriff's office. Tritt pounded on the door.

Across the street, Eddie Bly emerged from the Eatery, wiping his hands on his white apron. "You looking for the sheriff?" he called out.

Tritt paused and looked over his shoulder. "Sure am," he growled. "Is he in there?"

"He was an hour ago," Bly yelled back. "But he's gone off with Dolly Atkins."

"Well, where the hell does she live?" Tritt snapped. He crossed the street, approaching Eddie Bly. "I gotta talk to the sheriff and talk to him now."

"Now, Marshal Tritt," Bly said smoothly. "If I were you, I wouldn't go disturbing a man who's having an hour or two with Dolly. If you know what I mean. I reckon the sheriff will be back here at my establishment in another hour or so. I'll tell him you're looking for him."

"You do that," Tritt replied impatiently. He and his men mounted again and rode off in the direction of the perimeter guards. Eddie Bly stood on the porch and watched them go. When they were out of earshot and nearly out of sight, Fargo stepped out from behind the barrels.

Bly almost jumped out of his skin. "Mr. Fargo!" he said. "I'm glad to see you."

"Where's Dolly's house?" Fargo said. "You've gotta tell me. It's life or death."

"Oh, that new sheriff ain't at Dolly's," Bly said with a wink. "He told me to keep an eye out for you but to keep that Tritt fellow away from him. Follow me." The rotund fellow moved quickly, coming down the stairs and leading Fargo around the corner to a dark door on the side of the building. He knocked three times, and after a moment it swung open. Mike Ford stood there looking grim. He gestured Fargo inside.

The small storeroom was filled with crates. A dim oil lamp swung over a table with four chairs. On the table was a pitcher of water, a couple of glasses, and a bottle of whiskey. Eddie Bly left them to attend his restaurant.

"Sit down, Fargo," Ford said. He poured two glasses of whiskey and then raised one. "Glad to see you're in one piece."

"They tried to do me in," Fargo said, telling of the chase through the forest. The whiskey was rough as a porcupine's back, but it didn't matter. "So Jim Tritt may have figured out his cover is blown. Or at least that I'm onto him."

"Yeah," Mike Ford said thoughtfully. The dim lamp-light glittered on his star. He pulled a pocket watch out of his jacket pocket and glanced at it. From across the table, Fargo could see that inside was a picture of a girl and he saw Ford gaze at it for a moment before he snapped it shut and put it away. "We haven't got much time."

"And Jim Tritt's looking for you, too, Mike."

"This thing is bigger than I thought," Mike Ford said. He reached in his pocket again and pulled out a piece of paper. "Eddie Bly got a telegraph out this afternoon for me and I got an answer about an hour ago. Our Treasury investigators back East have been doing some footwork trying to figure this out."

"So, what's Tritt up to? And what's all this about the Goddard Gang? As far as I know, they're all still in prison for forgery."

"Right. Tritt's only half lying," Ford said. "All of them are dead or still in prison—except one. The forger himself, Alfred Doherty, the best forger in the world, maybe even in history. Before he and the Goddard Gang were caught, he'd apparently made up millions and millions of dollars of phony bills. They were hoarding them. But before the gang could circulate them, they were caught. We never found the counterfeit money. Alfred Doherty served his time and now he's a free man. But six months ago, the Treasury Department started seeing a few of these show up."

Mike Ford reached inside his jacket and pulled out two banknotes. He handed them over to Fargo, who turned them over in his hands.

"First Bank of Kansas City," Fargo read. "They look like good notes." The printing was fine-lined, with pictures of several buildings in Kansas City and serial numbers. "Looks legitimate."

"Sure does," Mike Ford said. "Lots of banks in the West issue their own notes. And they're legal tender.

Just as legal as this." Ford pulled two more notes from his jacket, federal Treasury notes. Fargo compared the picture of the former president Madison on the faces and the numbers and pictures on the back printed in green ink. The two were indistinguishable. Mike poured a glass of water and then said, "Dip 'em."

"What?" Fargo hesitated, then rolled up the four bills and dunked them into the glass of water. The water colored with running ink and he pulled them out. One of the Kansas City notes was a blur of color and one of the Treasury notes was a smear of green.

"They look pretty stupid, don't they?" Mike Ford said.

"Seems like it," Fargo said, laying the four bills out on the table.

"Actually, it's not as stupid as it looks," Mike Ford said. "This forger Alfred Doherty used water-based ink because it worked better. He'd drawn a replica of about thirty different kinds of banknotes and got some plates engraved. Using water-based ink, he could print them faster and they looked more real. The Goddard Gang was planning to flood the market with these bills, and by the time anybody got wise to it, they'd have already escaped the country. At least that was the plan."

"So who's passing these bad notes? The forger?"

"Maybe," Mike Ford said. "But they're turning up all along where Jim Tritt and his men have been."

"How'd Jim Tritt get ahold of these?" Fargo asked.

"I'm not sure yet," Mike said, gathering up the bills and pouring the water out on the dirt floor. He refilled their whiskey glasses. "The boys back East are checking out Jim Tritt. I should know more by tomorrow. All I know so far is he used to be a lawman of some kind. I guess he's looking for—"

"Alfred Doherty?"

"Sure. We know Doherty's somewhere in this territory."

"What's he like, this forger?"

"I was just a boy when Doherty was caught and sent to prison," Ford said. "But I've seen newspaper pictures of him. Flamboyant fellow, twinkle in his eye, could draw anything faster than lightning, always dressed like one of those fancy—hey! Fargo!"

Fargo was on his feet in a moment, cursing himself. How could he not have suspected? Of course!

"Over at the hotel," Fargo said. "No time to lose." Fargo opened the door of the storeroom a crack and saw that none of Tritt's men were around. He vaulted out, followed by Mike Ford. They hurried across the street and burst into the front door of the hotel. Mrs. Murphy, who was napping in her rocker, started awake as they ran through the lobby and pounded up the stairs.

Bethany's door was locked. Fargo swore and pounded on it, calling out to her. Then he stepped back and hit it full force. The flimsy lock gave way and the door flew open. The room was dark. And empty. The cotton curtains blew in the night wind at the open window. Fargo glanced out to see the roofline. Yes, they probably went that way.

Mike Ford felt the rumpled quilt on the bed. "No heat here. They've been gone awhile."

"Shit," Fargo said. So the innocent-seeming Asa Dalrimple, the "artiste" in his beret and his flowing silk scarves, was really Alfred Doherty, the most renowned counterfeiter in U.S. history. Goddamn. Fargo wondered if Bethany was in on it. She must know about her father's life of crime. He'd been in prison for twenty-five years. That's why she'd seemed so frightened when Jim Tritt and his men had come in hunting for somebody from the Goddard Gang. Sure, Tritt was looking for Alfred Doherty. He was looking for a man who could make him rich beyond his wildest imagination with the flick of his artist's wrist.

"What now?" Ford asked.

"Well, if Doherty and his daughter have headed out of town, they're going to need some luck to get by Jim Tritt's guards," Fargo said thoughtfully. "I'll get my extra ammunition from my room and then let's trail 'em."

Fargo fished out his room key and opened his door. He took two steps into the darkened room and then realized he was not alone. The thought flashed through his mind that in his haste, he'd been careless. He instinctively moved to the side just as the blow struck, a heavy swinging crash that would have cracked his skull and put him out for hours, but instead glanced painfully across the hard muscles of his broad shoulders.

Fargo turned toward his attacker, a dark form of a man behind the door. Mike Ford moved forward, through the lighted doorway. Another man came from the side, jumped Mike and they went down on the floor with a heavy thud, just as somebody else jumped Fargo from behind. As he hit the floor, Fargo's heavy fists and powerful arms lashed out in the half dark as he struggled with the two men who were trying to hold him down. A whistling right connected with a man's ribs and the air left him. He wheezed and loosed his hold on Fargo's neck. Fargo delivered a swift left uppercut in the direction of the other man's head and felt it connect with a bone-crunching impact. A third man was standing over him and lashed out with his boot, catching Fargo hard in the belly. For a moment red lights swam before his eyes, then with a roar, he leaped to his feet and pummeled his third attacker with a flurry of blows until the man sank to his knees. But there were others waiting in the darkness and they came forward, one by one, piling on top of Mike Ford, their fists lashing out of the darkness.

Fargo heard the click of pistols, saw barrels gleaming in the darkness, reflecting the light that was spilling in from the hallway. From downstairs, he heard Mrs. Murphy crying out for help and realized she'd been screaming for some minutes.

"Hold on." Fargo recognized Tritt's voice in the darkness. The dark forms of men got slowly to their feet. Somebody struck a match and lit an oil lamp. The room slowly swam in light. Downstairs, the old lady was talking excitedly to somebody. Fargo and Mike Ford stood up, side by side. Tritt and a half dozen of his men stood around the room. A couple of men had shiners, their eyes already swelling shut, and blood dripped from another man's split lip.

"What's going on, Tritt?" Ford shouted. "What the hell are you doing jumping a man in his own hotel room? I won't have this in a law-abiding town. And why the hell have you got guns on you? I told you no firearms inside town limits."

"Well, if it ain't the yellow sheriff," Jim Tritt said.

"Seems like we got a turncoat right in the middle of town." He nodded at Fargo.

"Turncoat?" Mike Ford said.

Fargo heard the hesitation in his voice. They'd have to play this just right. If they let on what they knew, Tritt and his men would gun them down in an instant. For a moment Fargo's fingers twitched and he calculated the odds. He heard voices from down below and heavy footsteps hurrying up the stairs. Eddie Bly and several of the Starkill men appeared carrying guns.

"What's going on here?" Bly said. "You need some help, Sheriff Ford?"

"Come on in, boys," Mike Ford said. "Marshal Tritt was just telling us that Skye Fargo is a turncoat. Now, how do you figure that, Tritt?"

"Because I know he's in cahoots with the old man," Tritt said, stepping up to Fargo until they were almost nose to nose. His eyes were colder than ice. "And I know the old man's got a girl with him, says she's his daughter. But Fargo and I know that ain't so. Fargo and I know that he's one of the Goddard Gang. And I know Fargo rode into town with the old man, took his horses over to the stable. You knew he was here all along, Fargo. Now, where is he?"

"I don't know what you're talking about," Fargo spat, thinking fast. "Sure, I met up with some old man and his daughter and took their horses into the stable. But if he's part of the Goddard Gang, then I don't know why you boys are so worried. He's just an old artist. Paints pictures. Totally harmless."

"You're causing all this ruckus for one old painter?

Well, he does sound dangerous!" Mike Ford said sarcastically. "He's the one who killed Doug Simpkinson?"

"Never mind," Jim Tritt said. "We got our reasons for hunting down this old man Doherty, er . . . Dalrimple. Fargo glanced at Ford and they exchanged a look at Tritt's slip. Yeah, Tritt knew Dalrimple was really the famous forger, Alfred Doherty. "Well, we'll catch 'em," Tritt continued. "I got this town sewed up tighter than a virgin's corset. Those two try to get out of here and they'll have to deal with Tritt."

"All right, Tritt," Mike Ford said. "But now you get your men out of here. And this is your last warning about guns. From now on, I'm going to deputize some men and station them at the edge of town. Starting now, you'll check your weapons there. But I want you and all your men out of Starkill for the night. We've had enough excitement for one day."

Tritt left in a fury, followed by his men. Several of them shot angry looks in Fargo's direction.

"I sure don't like that Marshal Tritt," Eddie Bly said when they had gone.

"Me neither," said one of the other men.

"There's something fishy about all this," Bly added.

"Yeah, it stinks," Mike Ford said. "Now, I need you men to help me out. There are some deputy stars in the desk drawer. About a dozen. Take 'em all and get some solid, dependable men. Organize yourselves to watch the roads in and out of Starkill. Keep Jim Tritt and his men from wearing their guns into town."

"It's sure strange telling a federal marshal he can't carry his gun, but sure, we'll do it," Eddie Bly said as the others nodded. "Is that all?"

"No," Fargo cut in. A plan had been forming in his mind. "Later tonight, maybe around midnight, maybe later, you'll hear a signal. One gunshot from the direction of the stable. When you hear that, start raising hell. Shout that you see somebody trying to get away into the darkness. Get as many of Tritt's men as you can to follow you. Get them all confused and keep them that way."

"A diversion, right?" Eddie Bly said.

"Exactly," Fargo said.

"We'll be ready," Bly said. The Starkill men trooped off.

"What have you got in mind, Fargo?" Mike Ford asked.

"Look, every day that Jim Tritt and his men hold this town hostage, it gets more dangerous. When we find Dalrimple—I mean Doherty—and his daughter, I want to get them out of town before Tritt finds them. It's either that or an armed stand with every man in town—"

"And that would mean a lot of casualties," Mike Ford said. "Tritt has a couple dozen trained men. A lot of innocent people would get killed."

"Exactly. I think we've got a better chance if we get the two of them out of Starkill. Once we find them, we'll get them horsed and give the signal. Eddie Bly can create the diversion. Tritt will follow but we can lose them, ride south to Cheyenne, and get some help. It's better than putting the whole town of Starkill in danger."

Mike Ford agreed and the two of them set off to find the missing artist and his daughter. With Jim Tritt and his men outside the town limits, they were free to conduct a house-to-house search. For the next three hours they knocked on doors, looked under wagons, peered inside barrels, poked in the stable hay, crawled through attics, opened closets, and talked to every man, woman, and child in the town of Starkill. Nobody had seen the missing pair.

The search had made everybody in town uneasy and everyone was staying awake to see what would happen. It was long after midnight, yet lamps were lit behind just about every dusty pane of glass in town. But all the searching had been in vain. The famous forger Doherty and his daughter had seemingly vanished into thin air.

"I guess we'll have to call off the search," Fargo was saying to Ford as they stood on the porch of the sheriff's office. At the distant end of the street in the darkness lit by a half-moon, he could see the figures of Tritt's men and others—Eddie Bly's group of Starkill men—also standing watch, awaiting a signal that had not come. As he watched, he saw a commotion and a knot of men, then made out the form of a wagon rumbling down the street toward them. A lone driver sat on the seat, hunched down, driving the one horse that pulled the empty wagon that jounced over the rutted street. Fargo could see the lines of extra traces tied over the horse's back.

"That's it," Fargo said quietly. He stepped down from the boardwalk, motioned for Mike to follow, and walked along behind the wagon as it bounced toward the stable. The driver drove the wagon in through the wide doors of the stable and brought it to a halt. He clambered down and lit a lamp, which he hung by a peg on the wall. Fargo stole up behind him, then spun him about and pinned him against the wooden side of the wagon. The man looked up and Fargo saw the scared and wrinkled face of an old man—but it wasn't Alfred Doherty.

"Who are you? Where did you take them?" Fargo shot at him, shaking him by the shoulders.

"My name's Paulie. Paulie Barkley. Uh, uh, I don't know who you're talking about," the old fellow started off, then he glanced over Fargo's shoulder to see Mike Ford standing there.

"That artist and his redheaded daughter," Fargo said. He let go of Barkley and stepped up to the horse, pulling off the lengths of looped traces, lines that had tethered two other horses to the wagon on the way out of town. Fargo walked to the back of the wagon and peered under it, then inside. It was empty, but he could see that the bottom was thicker than it needed to be. He opened the tailgate and knocked on the floor of the wagon.

"Hollow!" Mike Ford said.

"Look, I was just doing a favor for that artist," Paulie Barkley said hurriedly. "I mean, his daughter was scared by that marshal and all his men and he wanted to get her out of town. He said he had to get to California. So, he . . . he gave me some money and I smuggled the two of them out of town."

"Oh, hell," Mike Ford swore in exasperation.

"How long ago?" Fargo asked. "And where?"

"Couple hours. Left 'em by the side of the road about two miles out of town where the road bends and goes into the forest."

"I know the place," Fargo said. "Let's see the money he gave you."

"Huh?" Barkley seemed confused but complied.

Fargo took the bill, a U.S. note, licked his finger, and

rubbed it. He held it under the lamplight. The ink was indelible. He handed it over to Mike, who looked at it closely.

"Yeah, it looks real," Mike muttered.

"So, who's passing the bad bills? Jim Tritt, maybe?" Fargo saw Barkley's eyes widen.

"That would fit," Mike said. "He may have been a lawman once, but he's gone rotten."

"You're to say nothing about this," Fargo warned Barkley. "Nothing about smuggling those two out of town. Nothing about us or this money to anybody. Got that? Otherwise, we'll arrest you for aiding and abetting a criminal." Barkley's wrinkled hands were trembling. He was scared and he shook his head nervously. He'd keep his mouth shut.

"I guess it's time to give the signal," Mike Ford said.

They sent Barkley out of the stable, got their horses saddled up, and led them out the back way. When they had mounted, Fargo raised his Colt in the air and fired one shot.

The reaction took a moment. But suddenly there was the sound of great commotion from the edges of town where the main road led up from the south and passed through to the north. Fargo took off, leading Mike Ford through the dark backstreets, heading east, galloping through the small houses. In the distance, men were shouting and there was the firing of guns. Eddie Bly and the men of Starkill were creating quite a nice diversion.

Just as the houses petered out, Fargo caught sight of the dark beyond, a grassy meadow studded with rocks with a sheltering copse of short piñon pine on the far side. Fargo urged the pinto forward and then suddenly spotted a man's dark form rising up from a nearby boulder. A rifle barrel glinted blue in the moonlight. In an instant Fargo's Colt was in his palm; he fired just as the other man pulled the trigger. The bullet whizzed by his ear, missing him by inches while the man was flung back by the impact of a direct hit in the chest.

Their horses were galloping full out now, heading across the meadow toward the welcoming line of dark piñons. Behind them, Fargo could see the dark figures of men running along the perimeter of town. Hell, they'd been spotted. As their horses plunged into the trees, the shooting started, a hail of bullets that zinged around them, whining through the air. In another moment they were deep into the trees.

Fargo turned the Ovaro in the direction of the road, heading toward the spot where Barkley had said he'd left Alfred Doherty and Bethany. They rode the horses hard, dodging the trees, then hitting the road and galloping full out on the hard-packed earth. The half-moon hung low over the mountains to the west and the stars were ablaze across the black velvet sky. The rolling meadowland around was dark but alive with the rustlings and owl calls of the night. They'd taken a big risk running from the town. Jim Tritt and his men would be following close on their heels.

Up ahead was the spot where the road curved and entered the deep pine forest, the spot where Barkley said he'd left Alfred Doherty. When they reached it, Fargo dismounted and examined the ground. Mike Ford remained on his horse.

The tracks were there, plain as day, one long ridge where Barkley's wagon had scored the soft earth beside the hard-packed road, the grasses crushed as the three of them had untethered the horses and mounted up. Fargo searched the edge of the forest, looking for any sign of horse tracks in the soft pine-needle-strewn earth, in case Alfred Doherty and his daughter would have gone off through the woods. But he saw no traces of them having left the road. The minutes were ticking by as he searched along the road. Mike Ford waited. Fargo swore to himself, trying to imagine what Doherty would have done.

"My guess is they're going to stay on the trail," Fargo concluded. "If they're smart, they'll veer off at some point where their tracks could be disguised. If they're stupid, they'll stick to the trail."

He and Ford could ride along the trail at a walk during the long night, looking for tracks where the pair might have turned off into the woods, and waste valuable time. Jim Tritt was sure to catch up with them. Or else they could take the chance that the two escapees wouldn't think of doing anything so devious and were just riding along the road trying to put as many miles between them and Starkill as possible. Fargo thought for a moment and remembered coming on them the first time, the old man painting the sunset, Bethany incompetently lighting a smoky fire, the tent badly pitched. "Yeah, they'll be riding right down the middle of the road," Fargo said after a moment. He glanced up at Mike Ford and noticed he was holding his shoulder.

"I took a bullet back there," Ford said.

"Bad?"

"Not bleeding now," Mike said. Fargo could hear in his voice that it hurt like hell. "I can hold out."

They set off again, galloping hard. The miles flew by

beneath their horses as the road narrowed and became a winding track that skirted the dark forests, crossed the meadows, rippled up and over the low rocky hills. As they crested a hill, Fargo was just starting to worry that Doherty and Bethany had gotten smart, and that he and Ford might have galloped past their trail, when he spotted them up ahead. The moon had disappeared behind a mountain, but in the starlight, he could see the two riders. He and Ford urged their horses forward.

As soon as they heard the sounds of pursuit, Alfred Doherty, aka Asa Dalrimple, and Bethany increased their speed. Fargo could see them desperately laying their quirts across the horses' haunches. In a minute he and Ford were just behind them. As the distance between them dwindled, Bethany suddenly turned about and Fargo saw that she held a derringer in her hand. In an instant she fired and the bullet whizzed just overhead.

The Ovaro pounded the earth, pulling alongside Bethany's pitiful nag before she could fire again. Their horses were galloping side by side, his pinto holding back its speed to match the other horse's. Fargo reached over and made a grab for the pistol and wrested it from Bethany. She screamed and flailed at him desperately. Only then did she recognize him. He could see the surprise in her face as he reached across and plucked the reins from her hands. Their two horses came to a halt. Mike Ford rode toward them, leading Alfred Doherty's horse by the reins. Fargo was amused to see that even in their haste to flee Starkill, Doherty hadn't forgotten the tools of his trade. The big black artist portfolio was strapped to the side of the saddle.

"There's no time to talk now, Mr. Doherty," Fargo said.

At the sound of his real name, Doherty started, then made as if to slide down off his horse to make a run for it. Fargo's Colt was in his hand in an instant.

"Get back on your horse," he ordered Doherty. The old man froze and then obeyed. "Jim Tritt and his men are right behind us. I don't know what the whole story is, but you and I know they're looking hard for you. You got your choice. Come with Ford and me to Cheyenne. Or else I leave you here for Jim Tritt to find."

Bethany burst into tears. "Pa's gone straight," she sobbed. "Honest, Skye. We were just so scared. So we tried to run. . . ."

"All right," Fargo snapped. "We'll hear the rest later. Right now we've got to disappear." He glanced around and saw that the land to the east rose in a dark ridge of folded hills, and high above them were the snowy peaks of the Absaroka range. That country was twisted with deep canyons and gorges where they could lose their pursuers. Fargo glanced at Mike Ford, who nodded toward the east. They were agreed.

Fargo led off, with Bethany and her father following and Mike Ford bringing up the rear. The Ovaro set an easy pace down the road. Doherty and his daughter were riding nags that had been neglected for years. Their ribs stuck out, their coats were dull, and their bellies sagged. Fargo hated to see any horse in such poor condition. There was no excuse for it. But with those two nags, there was no way to outride Tritt and his gang. The only chance now was to lose them. Fargo's plan was to stick to the road for a while and then turn off where their tracks wouldn't be noticed. He kept his eyes open for rocky land, for streams, where they could travel and leave barely a trace.

It wasn't long before trouble found them.

The earliest hint of dawn was lighting the eastern sky when Doherty's nag suddenly went short. Fargo heard the horse stumble and looked back to see that it had slowed and was limping badly. Lame. He swore, called a halt, and dismounted.

"These damned horses," Doherty spat. "We bought these two just six weeks ago and they're always giving us trouble. If it's not one thing it's another."

"Shut up," Fargo snapped, suppressing the urge to punch the man for caring for his mounts so poorly. Obviously, the nags had suffered from a lifetime of abuse, but Doherty's lack of horse sense hadn't made things any better.

Fargo bent to examine the nag's front hoof and found a large stone wedged in the tender flesh inside the laminae. The nag whinnied in pain as Fargo removed it and saw from the swelling that it had been there awhile. He swore to himself. The nag had been in pain and had compensated by changing its gait. Now it would need a week's rest or more before it could gallop again. And meanwhile they were stuck. He thought fast. Time was passing, and with the coming of dawn, Tritt and his men would find it much easier to search for them. They'd have to leave the road now.

"We're going to split up," he said. "Doherty, get on my pinto. The nag will make better time without your weight." The old man slid down and did as he was told.

"What's your plan, Fargo?" Mike asked. His bullet

wound was obviously bothering him. He was holding on to his shoulder. "Hell, it's my shooting arm, too," he added.

"I'll get that bullet out of you tonight," Fargo promised. "Can you wait that long?"

"I'm not exactly looking forward to it, but yes," Mike said.

"Take Bethany with you and head straight into the Absarokas," Fargo told him. He pointed ahead to a slope of tumbled scree. "Use every trick you know to disappear. Meanwhile I'll leave a big messy trail leading off to the west. Tritt and his men will see the tracks of two horses and notice that one of them's lame. They'll figure they've got it made and might not suspect that there are four of us. It was too dark for them to see exactly who escaped the town on horseback and they might think we were Doherty and Bethany. I'll lead them on a goose chase and then circle back and meet you."

"Where and when?" Mike Ford asked. He pulled his pocket watch from his jacket and snapped it open.

Fargo squinted at the pale blue light in the east. "I make it about quarter past five."

"Twenty past," Ford corrected with a grin, snapping the watch case shut.

Fargo's lake-blue eyes scanned the terrain around them, the broad backs of the low hills, the jagged teeth of the distant peaks, the darkness of the deep pine woods. The light of the sunrise was pale pink on the distant peaks. He measured the distances, traced the route he would take.

"Make it about three this afternoon," Fargo said. He pointed to a distant foothill that rose up from the forested valley to the east. The hill was crowned with a circle of craggy red rocks like an eagle's aerie. "We'll rendezvous there. Up inside those rocks looks like a good shelter."

Mike nodded agreement. Fargo dismounted and watched as Mike led Bethany on her nag up the slippery slope of tumbled rock. The two horses climbed gingerly. With his booted foot, Fargo smoothed the earth where the horses had left the trail. He pulled off his neckerchief and swept it rapidly over the ground to obliterate any traces. When he had finished, he stood back to admire his handiwork. There was no way Tritt and his men would notice the faint traces that were left. He glanced up the slope and saw Mike and Bethany at the top. Mike gave a wave and they disappeared over the top.

Fargo took the reins of the lame nag and his Ovaro and led them a hundred yards back on the trail toward Starkill. There was a bare patch of earth, then a gently sloping bank where the pale green shoots of the summer grasses were just breaking through the yellow thatch and a wide-open high plain.

He mounted, Doherty behind him, and led their two horses off the road and onto the bank, leaving behind the obvious hoofprints like a sign pointing which way they had gone. Tritt and his men couldn't possibly miss it.

"Think it'll work?" Doherty said excitedly. When Fargo didn't answer, the old man spoke again. "Look, Mr. Fargo. I appreciate what you're doing for me and Bethany. I'm sorry I didn't take you into my confidence. But you see—"

"There's time enough for that later," Fargo said. This was no time for words. He put the Ovaro into a high lope across the plain. The nag kept up pretty well, freed from the weight of a rider.

Fargo felt a fury tugging at him that Asa Dalrimple, the artist, had been a fake, had not been who he said he was. And he wondered how much of a fake Bethany was, too. It was possible that Doherty had gone straight, as Bethany had said. It was also possible that they were still pretending and that he and Mike Ford were really helping two slippery criminals escape. Still and all, it was from Jim Tritt that they were escaping. Yeah, he'd get the whole story out of Doherty later when they camped. In the meanwhile he had to concentrate.

They had reached the far side of the wide plain, where some low hogback hills scalloped the edge of higher hills behind, when Fargo heard the sound he'd been expecting.

In the distance, from the direction of the road, the hoofbeats sounded like the low rumble of thunder. Fargo glanced back to see a plume of dust swirling up in the slanting rays of the rising sun. Tritt and his men had caught up to him faster than he'd feared. They were only a mile down the road at best. Hell, there wasn't much time to get out of sight. Fargo urged the Ovaro on, heading for a gap in the hogback hills, holding the reins of the nag.

They hurried faster now. And then it happened. The lame horse suddenly screamed and stumbled, jerking on the reins. It went down, sinking to its knees.

4

"I hear them coming, Fargo!" Doherty shouted.

Fargo didn't bother to answer, but slipped down off the pinto and ran back toward the nag. The pitiful horse was lying on its side, panting, its eyes rimmed white. The big black artist's portfolio had come loose and lay half under the horse.

"Come on," Fargo said under his breath, seizing the horse's bridle. The nag made an effort to rise, then sank back again. Fargo swore. There was no choice but to abandon the horse. The thundering hooves of their pursuers grew louder. Fargo got ready to mount the Ovaro.

"My paintings!" Doherty shouted, pushing him down. "I can't leave my paintings."

"Bullshit," Fargo said, starting to mount again.

"Please, I beg you," Doherty said, his voice trembling. He tried to get down off the pinto.

"Are you crazy?" Fargo yelled. With a curse, he ran to the downed horse and wrenched the big portfolio from under it, threw the object up to Doherty, and swung up onto the pinto. He was filled with fury now, fury at the idiot he was trying to save, a man who had been a crook and now was a crazy artist. Fury at their bad luck with the lame nag. Fury at Jim Tritt and his gang of toughs, whom he'd been following for two months and who were now hot on his trail.

The Ovaro leaped forward, its powerful legs pounding the grassy land, carrying them up the hillside toward the gap between the hogbacks. If he could just get out of sight, Fargo thought. Tritt and his men would see the tracks and know which way he'd gone. But they probably wouldn't pause long enough to determine how long it had been since he'd passed that way. They wouldn't assume he was only a couple of miles ahead. But if they spotted him, it would turn into a chase instead of a matter of following his trail. And the pinto, carrying two of them now, would have a harder time outrunning Tritt's gang.

Fargo glanced back just as he reached the top of the rise and saw the dark figures at the base of a swirling column of dust rising in the cool morning air. Then he drove the pinto down into the small valley that lay behind the hogbacks. He doubted he'd been spotted, but there was no time to lose. At the bottom of the coulee, a stream reflected the first rays of morning sun that poured in over the hogbacks. Fargo urged the pinto into the stream; even though it had not had water for several hours, it did not pause to drink, seeming to understand that every second counted now.

The surefooted pinto splashed up the brook, picking its way among the rocks until Fargo saw ahead a place where the stream split, one branch leading higher into the hills. He took the other, smaller fork, where the water ran in sheets over shelves of flat rock. The upstream branch seemed to open up into a larger canyon higher up. Ordinarily, it would be the perfect place to hide a trail and he would have brought the pinto out of the stream onto the smooth rock, where he would leave no tracks. But Tritt was too close behind; he would reach the spot before the tracks of the dripping pinto would dry in the coolness of the dawn. Fargo swore to himself, then had an inspiration. He dismounted in a flash, scooped up water into his hat, and tossed it onto the dry rock in splatters like a trail. That would confuse them. But what now?

On the other side of the stream, he saw ahead a gentle slope of broken gray rock. Up ahead on the hill near a stand of rangy cedars, a spring gurgled and spread out as it ran down the rocky hillside, wetting the rocks that shone darkly in the morning sun. Quickly, the pinto left the stream and took the slope, climbing the wet rocks carefully. Fargo glanced behind him into the small valley they were leaving behind. They reached the stand of cedars just as he saw the line of riders come up over the hill.

Fargo pulled the Ovaro farther into the stand of cedars until they were completely out of sight, and cautioned Doherty to remain utterly silent and still. The old man gripped his black portfolio and nodded. Fargo crept back to the edge of the cedars, drew his Colt, and peered out between the branches.

The riders, about a dozen of them, were coming up the stream in a long line. Three men were in the lead. The two on each side were scanning the banks for any tracks. In the center, he recognized Bruno Riker. Jim Tritt was nowhere to be seen. The riders arrived at the fork and called a halt, then broke up into two parties, one party taking the branch that led deeper into the hills.

A few minutes later Fargo smiled to himself as the remaining six reached the water he'd splashed on the smooth rock. They halted and all dismounted, drew their pistols, and then began leading their horses up the smooth rock, climbing in the direction of the valley above. They moved warily, looking all around them, listening. Yeah, they were pretty well trained, these men. Formidable foes. He'd been lucky this time, but he wouldn't want to underestimate them. Fargo waited until they were out of sight and earshot. He returned to the waiting pinto and Doherty.

Silently, he led the pinto through the stand of cedars toward the top of the slope until he was looking down into a forested valley of dark lodgepole pines. Farther to the north, he could just see the plain and the trail from Starkill where they had split up. In the far distance, he could see the low hill with the crown of red rocks where he planned to rendezvous with Ford. The sun was rising higher. Seven o'clock. Still early. They had plenty of time. He scanned the forest below. Easy to hide down there, he thought. But then, that's just what Tritt and his men would figure. The Starkill trail cut through the forest somewhere down there. And Mike Ford and Bethany were down there, too.

Fargo wondered where the rest of Tritt's men had gone. There had only been a dozen following him. As he set off, he knew there was every possibility that they were waiting somewhere in the forest down below.

When he and the old man were well inside the dark safety of the pine-carpeted forest, completely hidden by the thick pine trunks, Fargo followed the sound of running water and found a rocky stream. They dismounted and let the pinto drink and graze on the young shoots coming up on the banks. Fargo drank a long draft of the cold mountain water, then ate some pemmican from his saddlebag and gave some to Doherty, who grimaced but ate every bite.

When they were ready to set off, Fargo let Doherty mount, then he took the reins of the pinto and began walking.

"What are you doing?" Doherty whispered, seemingly awestruck by the silent grandeur of the forest.

"You ride. I'm taking this Indian style," Fargo answered. "On foot." It was easier to listen, to watch, to move silently on foot. And if a man was moving slowly, he could hear trouble coming from a long ways away.

After an hour they reached the Starkill road and crossed it warily, Fargo returning to obliterate their tracks with a switch of pine bough. In another hour, Fargo calculated they'd reach the rendezvous point an hour early. He was tired, he realized, having ridden hard through the long night. The pinto was holding up well, though. Fargo stopped often as they slowly traversed the forest and gave his horse plenty of time for grazing and fresh water. Alfred Doherty nodded himself to sleep and dropped his precious portfolio, then woke up with a startled cry. After that, Fargo tied the folio onto the side of the pinto and Doherty slept again.

The forest was peaceful, rich with game. From time to time he spotted the flash of white-tailed deer. As the sunlight slanted through the glistening green needles, a kit fox darted out of a chokecherry thicket, spotted him, and sped off. The occasional streams babbling with the release of spring were swarming with rainbow trout. The scurrying ptarmigans had lost their white winter color and were camouflaged again in browns.

As they neared the eastern edge of the wooded tract, the land began to rise very gradually toward the foothills of the Absarokas. The pines grew smaller and less stately, the soil rockier, and soon gigantic red boulders, some as large as small houses, rose around them. Fargo moved more warily now. This area was perfect for an ambush. But he had seen no one and heard no sounds of pursuit in the forest. Still, he moved slowly, pausing often to listen and to watch.

Alfred Doherty slept on and off, slumped down on the pinto. Occasionally, the old man twitched and called out in his dreams, but Fargo could not make out the words.

In a clearing, Fargo glanced up at the sun, then checked the direction of the shadows cast by the trees. He adjusted his own direction, heading a bit more to the south, which would bring them out of the forest just at the rendezvous point. A few miles on, the trees ended and a grassy field dotted with the huge red boulders lay before them. Above was the hill with its crown of craggy rocks. They could move from boulder to boulder until they reached the back of the hill and then they would climb up to the crown, an excellent lookout point. Fargo woke up Doherty, who blinked, sleepy-eyed, and mounted the Ovaro. Here in more open country, it made more sense to ride.

In another half hour they were around the back side of the hill and climbing toward the towering red rocks that rose like the turrets of a castle on the hill above them.

"That's spectacular," Doherty said quietly. "If only we could stop and I could paint it."

Fargo drew his Colt and continued up the slope as they neared the rocks, but there was no sign of movement. He spotted a gap in the rock circle and headed toward it. As they climbed the last few feet and entered the enclosure, Doherty whistled.

Fargo saw that he and Mike had chosen well. There was only one entrance to the rock circle and inside was a perfect grassy enclosure where they could hide the horses. The rocks were tall enough to hide the light from a campfire, and the stiff winds would blow the smoke away. He dismounted and climbed onto the rocks and looked down over the forested land they had just traveled through. Best of all, you could see anybody coming for miles. Yes, it was the perfect place to hole up for a needed day of rest before pressing on.

Fargo climbed down, took the saddle off the Ovaro, and gave it a good curry. The horse had had lots of water down in the forest and would be all right for a while. It began pulling at the yellow grass and chewing contentedly. Fargo patted its flank and returned to the lookout point. Doherty was opening up his portfolio and setting up his easel and a canvas, clearly intending to paint the spot. The midday sun was warm, but the stiff breeze blew cold. Fargo scoured the land below.

A couple of eagles flew in wide circles against a cloudless sky. Among the trees, from time to time, he caught the diamond sparkle of a stream. Otherwise, everything was quiet. Peaceful. And he was tired, dog tired.

Suddenly he started awake. Hell, he'd been asleep. In an instant he saw the sun was lower in the sky. It was close to six o'clock. Doherty lay fast asleep on the grass, a blanket from Fargo's saddlebag pulled over him. Mike Ford and Bethany were nowhere to be seen. What had awakened him?

There it was—the distant pop of gunfire. And again. Coming from down in the forest. Fargo leaned out over the rocks and peered down into the dark pines. It was impossible to see what was happening. It was bound to be Ford and Bethany and they were in trouble. Fargo made up his mind in an instant.

He whistled and the pinto came cantering toward him. He saddled it fast. The horse whinnied low, eager to be off. Doherty groaned and rolled over, then blinked awake to see Fargo sitting in the saddle.

"Jump up on those rocks and keep a lookout. When I get back, I want you to tell me if you saw any movement anywhere. Keep your eyes open."

Fargo headed out, the Ovaro moving fast down the back of the hill until they reached the cover of the big boulders. Then he rode carefully, eyes and ears alert, moving from cover to cover toward the edge of the trees. Ahead of him, he heard nothing. No sound of gunfire, no horses. Nothing. He entered the pines, scraggly at first, then denser as they rose taller to obscure the sky.

Then, with the instinct that had been honed by years in the wilds, he knew someone was nearby. Beside a large red rock, he brought the Ovaro to a halt and sat for a long moment in silence. The Ovaro silently shook its head. Yes, the pinto smelled something. He slid down. Colt in hand, he edged around the side of the boulder and looked into the dark tree trunks. Like a shadow, he moved forward a dozen yards, stopping behind a tree trunk. He peered out and saw another boulder ahead of him. On the smooth side facing him was a bloody hand-print. Even from this distance, he could tell by the bright red color that it was fresh.

Fargo looked around again, checking his back. He'd left the pinto untethered. The horse would stay where he left it unless he whistled. And if someone else stole up on it, it would whinny an alarm, then rear and run. But there was nobody at his back as far as he could see. Whoever was out there was straight ahead.

He moved forward now, taking cover behind the trunks, making a slow wide circle around the rock. Then he spotted it—part of a man's boot. There was some-body lying on the top of the boulder, lying in ambush. Fargo leaned down and picked up two small stones from the forest floor, checked behind him, then moved for-ward again. He was closing in on the rock now. Ten yards. Then five. He could no longer see the man's boot, but on this side of the rock, he saw the faint traces of blood, where the man had climbed up. There were crevices in the boulder that made the climbing easier.

Fargo tossed the first rock up and over the boulder and heard it fall in the forest on the far side. He felt rather than heard the waiting man stiffen with readiness. Then he threw the second and in an instant scrambled up the rock and seized the man's booted foot and pulled. Just as he'd hoped, the man came sliding toward him and they tumbled to the ground. Fargo pinioned the man's arms before he saw that it was Mike Ford.

"Fargo!" Mike said. He was in bad shape. Black blood darkened his shirt where he'd taken the bullet while es-caping from Starkill, and fresh scarlet stained his thigh.

His cheek had a deep graze, one eye was swelling shut, and his lower lip was split and bleeding.

"You look like hell," Fargo said. "Where's Bethany?"

Fargo immediately wished he hadn't had to ask the question. Ford's eyes glazed with rage and Fargo knew before he spoke that Bethany had been taken by Tritt and that Ford was blaming himself.

"She alive?" Fargo cut in before Mike could answer.

Ford nodded his head yes.

"How close are they?"

"I think they've gone. There were a dozen of them. They jumped us a mile from here. I took out four of 'em. Then I went down off my horse with this bullet and a bunch of 'em starting in on me. I played possum. They left me for dead. They're miles away by now." Mike hung his head, balled his fist, and hit the ground. "Hell, I should have fought back."

"Sure, and got yourself killed? That would have been real helpful."

"I should have—"

"Shut up, Mike," Fargo said. "You made the right decision. You're alive, aren't you? Trying to save Bethany would have been suicide. We'll get her back. Any more talk like that and I'll get real real clumsy when I start fishing out those bullets. Got that?"

Mike Ford nodded his head and, despite his pain, flashed a wry grin. Fargo helped him to his feet and was glad to see that Mike's leg wasn't hanging loose. The bullet probably hadn't shattered the bone. He whistled and the Ovaro came trotting toward them, its magnificent coat of white and black flashing among the trees.

"They got my horse, too," Ford mumbled as Fargo lifted him onto the pinto.

"I figured as much."

The blood from his leg wound was flowing pretty bad. Fargo managed to get a tourniquet on it and then Mike lost consciousness and slumped across the horse. Fargo led the Ovaro back to the edge of the woods and up to the rock fortress. All along the way, he thought about their situation. One old man, Mike badly wounded, one horse. A couple dozen—minus a few—tough men looking for them. And Bethany kidnapped.

Fargo kept looking behind him. Sure, Tritt and his men might have left Mike Ford for dead. But they might also have been smart enough to figure that Ford and Bethany were on their way to meet up with Alfred Doherty. And that was who Tritt was after. Fargo took care to leave a confusing trail, full of gaps and false starts. He took a long time returning, stopping here and there to gather firewood that he tied on the pinto behind the unconscious man. All the while he listened to the silence in the forest behind them. There seemed to be nobody following.

Doherty came running to meet them as they came into the rock circle. His face was filled with terror, his eyes wide, and his long white hair disheveled. Fargo pulled Mike Ford down from the horse and lowered him to the ground. Mike groaned, then lay still. His skin was paste white and he looked bad off.

"Bethany? Where is she?"

"Tritt got her," Fargo snapped. Doherty tore at his hair and stamped on the ground. It was a good thing Mike was still out cold and didn't have to witness Doherty's tantrum. "Save it. We got work to do if we want to get your daughter back."

But the old man seemed unable to control himself. He sank to his knees and began to sob. "You don't understand. She's all I've got. She's the reason I went straight. She's saved my life, oh, my poor Bethany, poor girl." Doherty wrapped his arms around Fargo's knees. "I don't care what you have to do. I don't care about anything else that Tritt might have got. I just want my daughter back. That's all I care about. Honest. That's all I want. I don't care about anything else."

Fargo had had enough. He hoisted Doherty to his feet and hit him hard across the face. The old man staggered backward, his eyes suddenly blazed with anger.

"Don't waste my time," Fargo shouted. "Every minute you blubber, Tritt's got your daughter. You want to do something? Get this wood unloaded and build a campfire over there under that overhang. Then get the pinto unsaddled. Now move."

Doherty jumped to do his bidding. Meanwhile Mike had begun to shiver and his eyes were fluttering.

Fargo pawed through his saddlebag and found a flask of Taos Lightning. He unscrewed the top—whew. Yeah, it was almost full. Even so, Ford was about to go through hell getting those two bullets out. He pulled the knife from his ankle scabbard and ripped an old shirt into bandage strips.

"Oh, hell. I need a needle and thread to stitch him up," Fargo thought out loud.

"I've got those," Doherty said. "I use them sometimes for stitching the backs on my canvases." He ran to his portfolio and soon returned with the needed items. Fargo brought out his two canteens, both full, and assembled everything on a rock under the overhang where Doherty was busy trying to lay the fire.

The old man had made a mess of it. A big pile of wood lay scattered about like the top of a beaver lodge; nearby, Doherty was trying, without success, to strike his tinderbox. Fargo cleared it all away and knelt down. In an instant he'd made a circle of stones and a neat tipi of branches with a mound of dry grasses stuffed inside. Fargo wrested the tinderbox from Doherty's hand and struck it near the grass. A small spark flew, then there was a wisp of white smoke and a tiny flame, which he fed with more grass until the logs caught.

"I see," Doherty said.

"Get the horse unsaddled. Then I want you to sit watch again." A thought struck Fargo. "Did you see anyone this afternoon while I was gone?"

Doherty shook his head no and left to take care of the pinto.

For the next two hours Fargo worked on Mike Ford. He gave him water until he came around, then made him drink Taos Lightning until he passed out again. There wasn't much he could do about the deep cut in Ford's cheek except clean it up with a splash of whiskey. The pain brought Mike around again and Fargo poured some more liquor down him. Meanwhile Doherty stood lookout and came to check on them from time to time.

The bullet in Ford's thigh had caused a lot of bleeding, and when Fargo opened it up again, another flood of fresh blood started flowing. But the bullet popped out almost immediately and Fargo stitched up the wound and bandaged the leg firmly. The shoulder was harder. The bullet was deep in the muscle and it wasn't budging. Fargo dug around for a while and the pain brought Mike awake. He groaned and finished up the last of the whiskey.

"Last try," Fargo said.

Mike looked up at him with glazed eyes. He'd groaned a few times through the whole ordeal, but he'd not cried out. "Gimme a stick," he rasped.

Fargo found a finger-sized twig, a strong one. With his good hand, Mike put it between his teeth. The knife bit deep again, slicing through the muscle. Fargo swore as his fingers felt for the bullet and finally located it, the hard knob buried in the flesh. Fargo pressed from behind. Mike's eyes rolled in his head, showing white, and his teeth clamped down. Just then the bullet gave way and eased out. Despite the stick between his teeth, Mike smiled. Then he spit out the twig.

Fargo stitched up the wound as best he could. He was no seamstress, that was for certain, but at least the edges of the flesh would stay together and heal. He bandaged the shoulder and fashioned a sling to hold the arm immobile. Then he propped Mike half sitting against a rock and built up the fire. He covered him with another blanket since he'd started to shiver again and had lost consciousness.

Fargo stood and stretched, the exhaustion coming in waves; except for a little pemmican, he hadn't eaten all day. Night had fallen. The wind blew cold this high up, although it was comfortable under the fire-warmed overhang. Doherty was still sitting at his post, although it had grown too dark to see much and the moon had not yet risen.

"Come on over by the fire," Fargo called. The two of them made a supper of the pemmican strips and hardtack from Fargo's supplies. Then he made a pot of coffee, which hit the spot. Afterward, as the moon rose, Doherty rolled himself up in a blanket and fell asleep. Mike was tossing fitfully, his forehead in a cold sweat. Fargo stoked the fire and sat in the lookout spot.

The moonlight made the dark forest below look like a vast ocean. Fargo scanned its edges, looking for any movement, any sign of danger, but he saw nothing. A small herd of deer ventured from the trees and grazed on the hillside, then disappeared again. The stars turned overhead. Fargo could feel sleep overtaking him. He wanted to keep watch all night, but he knew he had to get some rest if he was going to go on and if he intended to rescue Bethany. He'd scarcely had time to think of that. There'd be time enough the next day. He stumbled toward the fire, rolled himself into a blanket, and drifted down into blackness.

The sound of a lark awoke him. Fargo rolled over, smelled the sharp odor of the ashen campfire, then stood up and stretched. It was nearly dawn and he'd slept through the night. The pinto whinnied to see him awake. It was standing by the entrance to the rock circle, pawing the ground. For a moment Fargo imagined that the horse had stationed itself there to keep watch. He smiled to himself at the fantasy and thought it more likely the pinto was eager to get on the trail.

He dashed some water on his face, took a swig, and went to the lookout. The sky above was studded with clouds; far to the west he saw a bank of deep gray clouds piling up over the mountains. There was nothing to be seen below.

Doherty and Mike were still asleep. They were almost out of water—just half a canteen left—and short on firewood. And Fargo knew he'd have to get some food into Mike if he was going to recover his strength. He saddled the pinto and rode out, returning cautiously to the edge of the forest and to the spot where he'd found Mike. In the light of dawn, he carefully checked the area for any footprints other than his and Mike's, wondering if any of Tritt's men might possibly have tracked Mike after he crawled away from the ambush point. But no such prints were to be found. Nevertheless, Fargo used the last of the water to wash the traces of blood from the rock and he obscured their tracks as much as possible.

Then he rode deeper into the forest, stopping to water the Ovaro at a stream and to refill the canteens. At the edge of a marsh, he found some wild onions and herbs, and gathered up some rose hips that still hung on the branches from the previous fall. Through the trees, in the dappled light, he spotted movement—a herd of white-tailed deer. They were some distance off and he was downwind. They seemed to be coming in his direction, moving slowly as they grazed beside the stream. He hesitated, not wanting to use his pistol in case Tritt and his men were anywhere in the neighborhood. Instead, he pulled the rope from his saddle, slapped the haunch of the Ovaro, which moved off deeper into the woods. He crept forward toward the stream, hiding himself in a stand of chokecherry as he tied a lasso into the rope and knotted the other end around a tree.

Deer were damned fast, faster than a horse—even the

Ovaro—when in the trees. So his only chance would come if they wandered close at hand. A few minutes later they came into view, three does and two white-speckled fawns, along with a magnificent buck with a big rack. A fawn wandered within range and Fargo hesitated. Then the buck came closer, and stiffened, suddenly perceiving Fargo's man-smell.

In an instant the looped lasso was in one hand and snaking through the air. It fell, tangled in the prongs of the rack, and the buck reared. The does and fawns were gone in a flash of white. The rope tightened as the buck pulled, but it was caught. Knife in hand, Fargo leaped forward, then to one side as the doomed buck charged, head lowered. He threw himself against the buck and it went down, sharp hooves kicking. Fargo felt for the neck with his knife and in a moment it was all over.

Fargo untied the rope as the buck's blood spilled out onto the ground. He couldn't hoist the whole buck onto the Ovaro, or fix a travois, because it would leave a giant track as he dragged it back to the hill. On the other hand, he hesitated to leave a half-butchered deer carcass for Tritt's men to find. As he pondered the problem, he started removing the haunches and the shoulder joints. When he'd finished and tied the fresh meat onto the Ovaro, he stood up. He pulled branches from the choke-cherry bush and dragged over several large dead pine branches that had fallen. With these, he made a mound over the buck, which hid it pretty well. He washed up at the stream and started back.

It was noon by the time he returned. Doherty came running to meet him and Mike waved weakly from where he lay by the firepit. In an hour they had eaten spit-roasted venison and onions. With the rose hips, Fargo made a red tea, an old Shoshoni remedy, and fed it to Mike, who had regained some of his color but was still feverish. Then he sat with a cup of coffee resting by the fire. It was time to turn his thoughts to getting Bethany back. And to do that, he needed to find out everything Doherty knew about Tritt.

"I never wanted to do counterfeit money," Doherty explained. "I just fell in with the wrong crowd when I was a kid. But I swear to you I never passed one single counterfeit bill. I might've made lots of 'em, but I never tried to pass 'em off as real. That Goddard Gang got me in all kinds of trouble and then we got caught and sent to prison." The old man paused, and for a moment Fargo wondered if he was leaving something out of the story. Sure enough, Doherty added, "Uh, in prison is where I first met Jim Tritt."

"He was a prisoner?" Fargo asked.

"Nah," the old man said with a laugh. "He was the warden. Took a real dislike to me right off, and if I wanted to stay out of solitary confinement, I had to make him some money."

"What?" Mike Ford asked disbelieving. "Tritt, the *warden,* had you doing counterfeits."

"Sure," Doherty said. "Only he claimed they were like, you know, souvenirs, and he'd never spend 'em."

Mike Ford reached in his pocket and pulled out a few banknotes and passed them to the old man. "Did you make any of these?"

Doherty shuffled through them quickly. "Yeah," he said with surprise. "This one and this one are mine." He held them up to the light. "In fact, these are two I made for Tritt. I can tell by the serial numbers."

"So that explains the greenback trail you've been following," Fargo said to Mike. "Tritt's been passing off some of those phony bills while he's been hunting for Doherty. I guess he wants you to fix up some more for him."

Doherty flushed and tugged at his silk scarf. Again Fargo had the impression he was holding something back.

"You holding out on us?" Fargo shot at him.

"Holding out what?" Doherty shot back. "It's just like you said. Tritt's trying to get his hands on me. He wants to set me up like his own private mint. Minting money for him. But I won't. I've gone straight and I'm not going back to prison. Not for anything." He tugged at his white beard. "I know I've been a foolish old man. Only, we gotta get Bethany back. Please."

"We're working on it," Fargo said. He poured himself another cup of coffee and sat lost in thought for a while. With one horse between the three of them, it was clear he was going to have to leave Doherty and Ford here in the relative safety of the rocky aerie.

Climbing up on the lookout again, he checked out the forest. This time he spotted, far to the north, a smudge of smoke on the horizon. At first he thought it might be from Starkill, but he realized the town lay even farther north. No, it looked like a camp. Tritt's camp, most likely. He'd check it out at nightfall. There was nothing he could do until then.

Fargo napped during the afternoon and Mike felt good enough to prop himself up at the lookout. Doherty was too upset to paint and sat twisting his silk scarf by the black firepit. In the late afternoon, Fargo awoke, ate some cold venison, and saddled the pinto.

Three hours later he had found them. He'd secreted the pinto a half mile away in a thick copse of young pine and come forward on foot. Tritt's men had pitched camp in the middle of the forest beside a stream. It was a dumb place to camp because anybody could sneak up on any side and there were very few guards. Fargo found himself wondering if the men had set it up that way as a trap. Maybe they expected Fargo and Doherty to come after Bethany and were trying to trick them into thinking their mission would be easy. Tritt's men's horses were tethered singly to trees and not picketed or strung together. It made Fargo suspicious to see such trail-wise men making such blatant mistakes.

He stood still as a tree trunk among the pines, listening, watching. Then he moved forward inch by inch. The men seemed to be having a drunken party; they were singing and calling out to each other. Was it all a ruse to lure him in? Fargo checked behind him for the hundredth time. No. Maybe they were just being stupid, letting their guards down.

As he came nearer, he spotted a patch of live oak, like a waist-high carpet that spread out on one side of the camp. He crawled into it and then, yard by yard, came nearer, until he was just ten yards from the campfire. He peered out between the leaves, looking for Bethany, listening for her voice. But she wasn't by the campfire. Neither was Jim Tritt. But Bruno Riker was.

"—but the boss says we gotta find 'em," Riker was saying.

"Too bad Tritt didn't leave that little redheaded chickadee with us so we could have some fun tonight."

"Yeah, why should he get all the fun?"

There was a roar of drunken laughter, then another voice.

"But the boss said to find 'em and kill 'em." Riker again.

"Let's not and say we did!"

"Tritt wouldn't like that none."

"Oh, come on, Bruno. Why should we kill ourselves trying to find that old geezer when the rest of our gang is heading up to get the goods?"

"That's right!"

Fargo wondered what they were talking about. One of the men tossed some more wood on the fire and it blazed up. He could see them all very clearly now.

"Tritt don't give a damn about that old man."

"We got orders to find him and kill him." Riker spoke haltingly, but he was sticking to his guns.

"Besides," another voice cut in, "how do we know the rest of 'em ain't going to get that money and then cut and run? How do we know we're going to get our share?"

A few more men shouted the same sentiment. Fargo listened carefully to the babble of voices, trying to separate out the words from the noise.

"Yeah. Once we got the map off that girl, we got it made. That's all we was after! Now we're gonna be rich as kings!"

The men gave a drunken cheer. Bruno Riker shouted over the crowd trying to quiet them, but they turned on him, taunting him. And then a few of the men jumped him. There was a scuffle and it took five men to get Riker down.

"Look, Riker," one of the men shouted, "I'm not going to let my chance to be a millionaire slip through my fingers. No sir. And if you don't cooperate with us, we're going to slit you open gut to throat and tell Tritt that the Trailsman caught up with you. Are you in with us or against us?"

Fargo saw Riker reluctantly nod his head.

"All right," the man continued. "In the morning, we're going to ride out of here. We're going to follow Tritt and catch up to him, tell him we found Fargo and the old man and we did 'em in. By the time Tritt finds out the truth, I'm going to be down in Mexico with a señorita on one arm and living high on the hog."

The other men cheered and danced around the fire, passing the bottles of booze. Fargo cursed Alfred Doherty. The silly fool still hadn't told him the truth. Obviously there'd been a map that Bethany had been carrying with her. And the map showed the location of a stash of counterfeit bills. Millions and millions of dollars' worth from the sound of it. Probably they were the bills that were never found when the Goddard Gang was stuck in prison. And all those years, Alfred Doherty knew just where they were. Fargo swore softly to himself and retreated through the scrub oak.

He withdrew a short distance away from the camp and considered the horses. Camp discipline had completely broken down. Not a guard remained on duty. So getting the horses away was not a problem. But in the morning, the men would know somebody had been horse stealing. And that would lead them to suspect that Fargo and Doherty had paid a visit. He didn't want to take a risk that the men might reconsider their priorities and decide to continue their search instead of jumping ship. Then he had an idea. He returned to the Ovaro and removed the blanket from under the saddle, then wrapped it around him. It was an old Indian trick, disguising the human smell so the horses wouldn't get stirred up.

It took him ten minutes of slow forward movements before he was standing among the tethered horses. Some of the men were still lounging around the campfire, passing the liquor. Others had fallen asleep and were snoring loudly.

With a whisper, the knife was out of his ankle scabbard and in his hand. He selected a fine muscular sorrel and then spotted Mike's strong gruello. Yeah, those would be fine. Just for the hell of it, he chose a fine gray, too. Fargo moved slowly among the horses, wrapped in the horse blanket that reeked of the pinto's sweat. The animals barely stirred as he sliced the rawhide tethers of the three horses, then bent and chewed on the remaining end, tearing it with his teeth. Yeah, that would do. He untied a few of the other horses and left the tethers dragging on the ground. In another half an hour he'd gotten the three horses spirited away, tied in a string, and hidden with the Ovaro. Now for the rest.

He sprinted through the dark forest in a wide circle to the far side of the camp and stopped, took a deep breath, put back his head, and howled like a wolf. Once, twice, and again. Any Shoshoni, for instance, would have known in an instant it was a human call. But Fargo was counting on the fact that none of Tritt's men was part Indian. He went another quarter way around the camp and howled again. Then he came in closer.

The wolf howls had had the desired effect. Fargo could see that the three men who remained awake had thrown a few more logs on the fire and were huddled around. Nobody was near the horses, though. Fargo moved up close to the horses again, still wearing the blanket. Then suddenly he removed it and flapped it in their direction. The horses woke and panicked. The ones he'd untethered reared up and took off. The men shouted by the fire. Fargo retreated into the woods, ducking behind a tree just as a bullet whizzed by. He yelped a few times like a wolf that had got winged.

"Hell!" one of the men shouted. "Damn wolves run off some horses." There was a flurry in camp as the men prepared to go after them. Fargo returned to the pinto and led the string in a wide circle through the night-dark forest and back up the slope to the rocky stronghold.

Yeah, things were starting to look up, he thought. Now they had horses and they could go after Tritt and his men. But fury rose in him. Hell, he hated to be lied to. He'd been putting his life on the line trying to get Doherty and his daughter away from Jim Tritt, and all the while the old man had been lying to him. Fargo's fists closed hard around the reins as he climbed the final slope. He couldn't wait to get his hands on the old man now.

Mike woke immediately when Fargo rode in with the horses and stood up, limping toward him as he dismounted. The fire was a low gleam of red embers and Fargo could see Doherty's sleeping form under a blanket beneath the rock overhang.

"You did it, Fargo!" Mike said, clapping him on the shoulder with his good hand. "Hey, you even got my gruello back." The blue came over and nuzzled Mike.

"Yeah, well, what I found out was real interesting," Fargo said. He stalked over to the campfire and threw a couple of logs on the embers. They caught fire and blazed up. Then he leaned over and yanked the blanket off the old man, then kicked him. And not lightly either. Mike had come up behind him and stood watching, curiosity in his face.

"Get up."

Doherty came awake and sat up, frightened.

Fargo grabbed his collar and hauled him to his feet. "Now it's time for some straight answers. What were you planning to do with the *map*, Doherty?" Fargo yelled at him. "Yeah, you heard me. The map! What was your plan? Go rescue all that counterfeit money yourself? Make yourself a rich man? Return to your life of crime?" He pushed the old man down onto the ground where he cowered.

"A map?" Mike said coolly. "And a stash of counterfeit money. Sounds like the Goddard Gang bills that were never recovered."

"Sounds like that to me, too," Fargo said. He pulled the Colt from his holster. It was time to scare the old man into honesty. He'd had enough of all the falsehoods and fakery.

"The map—yes, the map," Doherty stuttered. "Yes, I didn't have a chance to tell you about that—you see—"

"I don't think we should let this lying son-of-a-bitch live another moment, do you?" Fargo said with a wink at Mike as he spun the barrel of his Colt.

Mike drew his pistol and cocked it. "He's been lying the whole time we've been trying to save his skin," he said. "Lying about everything."

"I'm not lying now!" Doherty said, groveling at their feet. "Please, please. I'll tell you everything. The map, yes, the map. It belonged to Finch Goddard, head of the gang. I never knew where they had buried all the bills they forced me to make for them. Honest, I never knew. But then when Finch died in prison, he gave me the map. Made me promise to take it to his old girlfriend when I got out. Honest. He said she'd always wanted to be rich and that's why he'd started the gang. He knew if she had the map, she'd be tortured by all that money lying up there waiting to get rescued. He said that would be his last revenge on her."

Fargo barked a laugh, echoed by Mike. "Sure," Fargo said. "Some fairy tale."

"No, honest," Doherty said. "I know it sounds crazy, but it's true. Six months ago, when I got out of prison, Bethany and I went straight up to Ogallala. Only we found out Finch Goddard's dove had been dead for ten years. I didn't know what to do with the map. I should have burned it. Only I didn't. We hid it in Bethany's corset."

"And that's what Tritt's been after all along," Fargo said. "The map to the counterfeit stash. How did he know you had it?"

"He'd heard a rumor from some of the other prisoners," Doherty said. "and the day I got out was the day he quit as warden. I knew he was following me. But I thought I'd lost him back East."

"But he's been following you, collecting a bunch of

men with the promise of becoming rich. And meanwhile he's been leaving a greenback trail of bad bills," Fargo said.

"And that's what put us onto him," Mike said.

"You know where this stash is?" Fargo asked Doherty. The old man nodded. "Then we'd better saddle up and get riding. The way I see it, we've got one chance now. We've got to beat Tritt to the treasure, and then use it to buy back Bethany."

"But if those bills get out on the market, or even a rumor of them," Mike said, "there'll be a panic. We can't take that chance, Fargo."

"Well, we'll figure that out somehow. Let's get going."

In ten minutes they'd broken camp and were about to mount, Mike and Fargo riding bareback, the pinto's saddle on the sorrel for Doherty. They'd be riding full speed, so Fargo had taken all the supplies and wrapped them in the blankets, strapping the aparejos to the gray.

"So, where's this stash located exactly, Doherty?" Fargo asked, swinging up onto the pinto.

"Why, it's buried up at a place called Colter's Hell," Doherty replied.

Fargo laughed. Of course. It would be Colter's Hell. No wonder Bethany and her father had reacted so strangely when Fargo had first mentioned the place. They set off as the moon was lowering toward the west. There was a long ride ahead of them. And every minute counted.

5

It was dawn when they'd passed miles to the west of the town of Starkill, the last white settlement for a couple hundred miles in the direction they had taken. All the long day they rode continuously, heading north through the forests and across the wide plains, then angling to the northwest. The horses galloped until exhausted, then stopped for water, cantered for miles, then galloped again, heading toward the mysterious land called Colter's Hell.

All the way, Fargo kept a keen eye out for any trace of Jim Tritt and his men, but saw nothing. There was no trail up to Colter's Hell. So Tritt might have gone any of a hundred ways. He might be riding fifty miles to the west of them. Or they could run into him just over the next rise.

The wide earthen tracks gave way to narrow game trails, and then they were bushwhacking, making their way through trackless countryside, mile after mile. They paused for a brief rest at sunset, then pressed on for another few hours, riding more slowly in the darkness the length of a huge valley that stretched south to north. When they reached the head of the valley along about midnight, Fargo called a halt and they rested without a campfire at the foot of a cliff. Before dawn, Fargo roused them and they set off again. They were making good progress. At this rate, they'd be entering the land called Colter's Hell by the next morning.

During the long hours of riding, Fargo had time to think of Bethany. He wondered how bad she was getting treated. Tritt had wanted Fargo and Doherty killed by the men he left behind. With Doherty dead, Tritt could have assumed his counterfeits would remain a secret and he'd have just enough time to get them exchanged for real goods and money before someone just happened to spill some water on them and discovered they were fakes. By that time he and his men would be safely out of the country, living like pashas, just as Finch Goddard and his gang had planned.

Fargo noticed that the landscape was growing stranger. This was land where white men rarely ventured. The Lewis and Clark expedition had passed to the north of this land. Then a discharged member of the party, John Colter, ventured deep into the back country and no one had believed his reports of the strange sights he saw. The peaks grew higher and more jagged. They crossed splendidly broad rivers that had names only known to the Shoshoni and the Blackfoot tribes. Fargo kept his eyes open for Indians, but the land seemed empty of all human beings.

The second night they stumbled on a cave large enough for them and for the horses. They were well out of the cold night wind. Again, they had no fire. Fargo didn't want to risk attracting attention either from Shoshoni or from Tritt. So they made do on more pemmican, some dried berries, and water from the canteens. Before dawn, Fargo left the others sleeping in the cave and took the string of horses down toward the stream he heard babbling below. There was a musty smell of sulfur in the air, and as he neared it he saw a fog rising up from among the trees, hovering over the running water. He continued to the edge of the stream and let the horses go to drink. The Ovaro shook its head in protest.

"Don't like the local brew?" Fargo asked the horse, then knelt and cupped his hand. The water was warm. Actually hot. The fog was a result of the steam rising from the hot spring. Fargo dashed the water over his face and neck, then filled his canteen full of the hot stuff and returned with the horses to the cave. He'd find some cold water for them later. Meanwhile he used the hot water to make some coffee; it came out tasting like lukewarm rotten eggs, but Mike said it was better than no coffee at all.

Just as first light was spilling into the valleys, they hit the trail again. They were traveling up a canyon choked with cottonwoods and willows, the buds just bursting into yellow leaves. They were riding along the bank of the stream when Fargo felt the hair prickle on the back of his neck. The pinto shook its head uneasily. Fargo turned around and caught Mike's gaze. Yeah, Ford felt it, too. Something not quite right.

They halted for a minute and Fargo sent Mike and Doherty on ahead while he took the pinto into the willow thicket and tethered it there. Moving slowly through the underbrush, he retraced their steps a few hundred yards and then paused, well hidden in the branches. He waited, listening to the rush of crystal water and the whisper of cottonwood branches. Ten minutes later he spotted him. Moving like a deer along the stream, a

Shoshoni. An old brave, his hair two silver braids, his compact body hardened by a life in the wilds. He was wary and cautious as an old wolf. As Fargo watched, the brave stopped and looked around. The Shoshoni sensed his presence just as Fargo had sensed the Shoshoni's. The Indian melted into the willows and was gone.

Fargo waited a moment and then stood up noisily, rising above the thicket, making no effort to be subtle. He had no doubt the brave was watching him from cover. And if the Indian had wanted to kill the three of them, they'd be dead men already. The Shoshoni was just being careful. And so was Fargo. Knowing he was being watched, he raised his hand and made the Shoshoni signal for *friend*. He held it up for a long moment, then turned and retraced his steps to the pinto.

He had just mounted his horse when the sound of gunfire erupted from upstream, from the direction Doherty and Ford had taken. Fargo pulled his Sharps rifle from the saddle scabbard and spurred the pinto forward. It sprang upstream, splashing through the water and pounding up the banks, dodging the big tree trunks and plunging through the thickets. The canyon walls were closing in, the passageway getting narrower to a point just ahead. He burst through it and came to an open clearing and saw before him the thin ribbon of a narrow waterfall. There was no way out. And then he knew he'd made a mistake. Maybe a fatal mistake.

"Freeze!" a gruff voice said from behind him. "We gotcha covered."

All around the clearing, Fargo's quick glance took in the forms of a dozen men hunkered down behind rocks and trees, men who were bristling with rifles, hidden in the crevices of the rocks behind him that he'd just passed through. There was no way back either. In the center of the clearing, Doherty knelt down on the ground, hunched over the form of Mike Ford. The old man was holding Mike's head in his lap and fresh blood darkened the earth around them. Fargo could see that Mike was dead. The rage rose in him then, welling up in black waves, coursing through his body like a bolt of lightning.

"Get off your horse. Throw down your guns. You've had it, Fargo." The voice was Jim Tritt's.

In a flash, Fargo whipped around in the direction of Tritt's voice. If he was going to die, then Jim Tritt was going down to hell with him, he decided. From behind the cover of a rock, he spotted the ebony gleam of Tritt's greased-back hair, took in the dark eyes sunk deep in the thick face, while in the same instant he brought his Sharps around fast and fired.

Tritt's head disappeared and a scream of agony came from behind the rock. Fargo cursed. Hell, he'd not blown the bastard's brains out as he'd hoped. Tritt's men were frozen in disbelief. Fargo leaped down off the pinto and slapped the horse away from him to get it out of the cross fire. Doherty got to his feet and raised his hands in the air.

"Don't shoot! Don't shoot!" The old man dove for cover behind a rock. Fargo looked around. There was nowhere to hide. He was completely exposed. From behind the rock, Tritt screamed again, a mixture of pain and rage.

"*Shot—my—goddamn—ear—off!*" Tritt shrieked. Despite the situation, Fargo grinned. "Get—the—bastard's—gun."

"Skye! Pa! I'm over here—" The voice was Bethany's, but Fargo couldn't see where she was. She was shut up immediately, as if somebody had clapped a hand over her mouth.

Anticipating their moves, Fargo hit the ground just as bullets flew overhead. He spotted a long, boulder crawled toward it, then vaulted over, taking a bullet in the calf. Fargo gritted his teeth at the explosion of pain and the hot gush of blood. Hell, this was some fix, pinned down by a dozen men, shot in the leg. It looked like his luck had finally run out.

A skinny man dashed from behind a tree trunk, heading for a rock, and Fargo plugged him in the chest. He went down. He'd take as many of Tritt's men with him as possible. A bald man suddenly popped up from behind a rock and fumbled with his trigger. Fargo beat him to it, blowing his head open. He paused and reloaded.

"Give—up—now—Fargo," Tritt screamed out.

Fargo could hear the pain in his voice. Yeah, it hurt like hell to lose an ear. He just wished he'd aimed better. Or that he could get one more shot at Tritt. Just one more. Dead center.

They had him for sure, Fargo realized. Already he could see Tritt's men trying to move around to get him surrounded, to catch him around the back of the log. He popped up and got another man as he dashed from rock to rock. And just then a bullet screamed over his head, missing his scalp by less than an inch, carrying his hat off into the air. Fargo hit the ground again and Tritt's men cheered. There were too many to keep them all covered. He was done for. He knew it and they knew it.

He thought fast and unbuckled his gun belt, slipped the Colt out of his holster and into the belly of his shirt. Yeah, just one more clear shot at Jim Tritt. That was all he wanted. A last wish. He slipped the neckerchief off and stuck a corner in the barrel of his rifle, then lifted it high.

"Giving—up—Fargo?" Tritt's voice called out.

"You got me, Tritt. Let's negotiate for the girl."

"Ha! Negotiate? What you got to trade?"

Fargo thought fast. "Information."

"Oh yeah? Like what kind? I got a map. I got the girl and the old man. And I got you pinned down like a butterfly. Seems like I got all the information I need."

Tritt's men laughed.

"Information about the money you're going to dig up," Fargo called out. "That guy you just killed was working undercover for the U.S. Treasury."

That got Tritt's attention. There was a long silence.

"So what?"

"So before we left Starkill, he cabled to the Treasury to be on the lookout for a certain kind of banknote. A certain banknote that Doherty made a long time ago. They're sending word out to every bank and town and store in the territories. Might be the First Bank of Kansas City. Or it might be a note from the United Bank of Nevada. You and your men try to pass one of them, you're going to be caught in a minute. And the Treasury will run the whole lot of you down."

Fargo paused. Hell, it was a lousy lie, but maybe Tritt would buy it.

"So you're saying there's just one kind of banknote that's no good?"

"That's right," Fargo said. "And I know which bank it is. You let me walk out of here with the girl and Doherty and I'll tell you which one. Give me your word and I'll throw out my rifle." Yeah, that was it. He knew Tritt would never keep his word, never let them go free. He wondered what would happen to Doherty and Bethany once he was dead, but he put the thought out of his mind, concentrating on getting Tritt to walk into the trap. And then Fargo would get his last wish. There was a long pause.

"Throw out your rifle, Fargo!"

"I got your word?"

"Sure. Sure, Fargo. Seems like a fair trade."

Fargo threw the Sharps over the log.

"Don't, Skye—don't—" It was Bethany's voice again.

"Stand up. Let me see you."

Fargo got to his feet. His gun belt lay hidden by the log and the Colt was in his shirt, the bulge hidden by his leather vest. His calf hurt like hell. But in a little while he wouldn't feel a thing.

"All right Fargo, walk forward."

Fargo took a painful step forward, then another.

"How about you, Tritt?"

Tritt appeared from behind the rock. In front of him, he held the struggling form of Bethany. Her auburn hair was a wild nest around her scared-pale face. Fargo could see that Tritt had knotted a plaid shirt around his head to stop the bleeding from his ear. But the former warden knew all the tricks of using a hostage as a shield. He wove from side to side and was careful not to let any part of him show for long. He thought Fargo had no gun, but he was still being cautious. Hell, by the time Fargo could pull the pistol from his shirt and aim it, he might be a dead man. It would be impossible to get a clear shot at Tritt without hurting the girl. Tritt moved forward and his men all stepped out from cover and began closing in on him, rifles trained on him, assuming he was unarmed.

"Let me get the girl and Doherty on horses and out of here," Fargo said. "Then I'll tell you what you want to know."

"Sure," Tritt said smoothly, coming nearer.

Fargo's right hand twitched, eager to have the Colt in it, aching to drill a neat hole right between Jim Tritt's sunken eyes. They were closing in on him like a pack of wolves.

In a flash, Fargo saw his chance. He took another step forward, then stumbled as if in pain, and as he dove, he pulled the Colt from his shirt and aimed at the side of Tritt that was suddenly exposed, hoping the bullet would go up through the chest and find the heart. The shot exploded, and as Fargo hit the ground, he realized the shot had gone too low. As he rolled over from the impact, he saw Tritt drop Bethany and clutch his middle. Bethany screamed and sank to the ground.

Fargo rolled to his side and aimed again, straight at Tritt's heart, but just as he pulled the trigger, one of Tritt's men reached him and a booted foot caught his upraised hand. The shot went wide and the Colt flew from his fist. Fargo swore to himself as Tritt's men began pummeling him with their rifle butts, kicking him with their sharp-toed boots.

Yeah, they'd beat him to death now. This was the way

he was going to die. He felt his ribs break and felt some-one stomp on his wounded calf. He closed his eyes and gritted his teeth. He wouldn't give them the satisfaction of crying out. He let his mind grow dark, felt the waves of agony wash over him as if from far away, felt the pain radiate from his groin, from his shoulders, his neck. He drank the silvery taste of his own blood in the back of his throat, felt his insides shift inside him at the impact. Pain. It was only pain, he told himself. Death would come soon and relieve him.

He heard a voice calling him back. The blows had ceased but the pain was still there, and he felt as if he were floating on a dark ocean. Waves carried him up and down.

"Fargo—tell me—which banknote." Tritt's voice came in gasps. "Which—is it? Then I'll—let you live."

You won't let me live. Fargo heard his own voice in-side his head. He willed his lips to move. With his last ounce of strength, he willed himself to tell a last lie, to have a last revenge on Jim Tritt.

"All of them," he croaked. "All of them." He heard his voice from a distance and it sounded like a stranger's. "The Treasury's got a list of the banks. The notes are no good. You lost, Tritt."

It was a damn lie, but Tritt bought it. There was a howl of fury and Fargo felt the jolt of the blows rain in on him again. He felt himself sinking into the darkness and he thought at least he'd shot off Tritt's ear, put a bul-let in his hip, and made him think the counterfeit bills were no good. If only he'd been able to get Bethany free. This was it at last. The end of the trail.

He let himself sink down into the warm and painless dark, where there were no thoughts and no regrets.

Wood smoke. The thought entered his mind and then blinked out. A long time later. But what was a long time? He was floating in warmth and then he felt a prickle of pain. Then a rushing ache through his spine. He cried out and the blackness came on again. Again and again, he came up from the shadowy depths as if washed ashore on a beach, only to be swept away again by the waves. Fargo. That was his name. Yes, he remembered. Tritt, Jim Tritt, a man with sunken eyes and greased-back hair, the small valley with a thin waterfall. He sank again.

Hot water on his skin, then the cool air. Stinging. His eyelids were like mountains, impossible to move. He tried pushing against them. Someone was there, moving near him. Hot water again, the smell of burning herbs. He inhaled and entered the blackness for a timeless time.

Orange flames danced. He watched, then realized his eyes were open, that he was lying on his side staring at a fire. The scene swam into view, but he could only see with his right eye. He tried to move his hand, but it felt nailed to his side. Then it came up to his face, slowly. Bandages covered his head and the left side of his face. He felt along the side of his ribs, tracing the heavy folds of fabric that felt as if they were keeping his insides from spreading out. It hurt to breathe.

He was lying in a small room, round, a tipi. A face swam before his eyes, a woman with a face like the moon, round and placid. Almond eyes and long braids.

Shoshoni. She smiled to see him and her eyes were merry.

Thank you, Fargo said in Shoshoni. Then realized his lips had not moved. He tried harder. "Thank you," he repeated, and this time he heard his voice. She laughed and patted his shoulder. He slept again.

The next time he awoke, he struggled to sit up. She came to him immediately, helping him. The pain was excruciating, but he fought it, knowing he was going to live, his body was healing. After a few minutes of effort, he was sitting upright, propped against a pile of buffalo skins. The daylight filtered through the skins of the tipi. Totems—stuffed birds and drums of stretched skins with dangling eagle feathers—hung from the sides of the tipi. Fargo knew enough about the Shoshoni to realize he was lying in the tipi of the tribe's medicine man.

The Shoshoni had strong medicine. He'd been lucky to survive the beating and luckier still to have been found and taken in by the Shoshoni. They weren't always friendly to white men.

The Shoshoni woman brought him a cup of something hot that smelled of pine pitch. He sniffed it and wrinkled his nose, but she indicated that he should drink. It burned on the way down but then felt like it radiated throughout his body and he felt clearheaded. He smiled at her.

"Name?" he asked in her tongue.

"Kimama." Her eyes were like two bright black jets in her full face.

"Kimama," Fargo repeated. He knew the word meant butterfly and he raised his hand and made it flutter in the air. She laughed at that.

"And you are Eagle-on-Wind," Kimama said. Fargo was surprised at the familiar words and searched his mind for the name. Then he remembered Istaga, the Shoshoni brave he had met on his way to Starkill.

"You know Istaga." Fargo laughed. "Coyote Man. Is he of this tribe?"

Kimama laughed again. "Istaga is my brother."

He'd been damn lucky, Fargo thought. The Shoshoni could just as well have left him for dead. But Istaga must have been the one to find him. And they'd taken a lot of trouble to fix him up.

"Now you must rest," Kimama said firmly.

It was many days before he felt strong enough to stand. And all the days of his recovery, only Kimama came into the tipi. While he had been unconscious, the Shoshoni healers—whoever they were—had removed the bullet from his calf, clamped his wounds shut with thorns, and bandaged his midsection and limbs to give them a chance to heal. Every day Kimama brought something new to feed him. First herb tea, then broth, then gruel and meat stew. He could feel himself gaining strength daily. He stretched his muscles again and again, easing them back into usefulness. It was slow and painful work, but he knew it was necessary. He tried not to think about Tritt, about Bethany, Mike Ford, and Alfred Doherty, but to concentrate his mind on getting better.

A week after he regained consciousness, Kimama removed the bandages from his face and head. He decided to try to leave the tipi. Slowly, he crawled out of the flap, into the sunlight, and staggered to his feet. A circle of Shoshoni women stood watching him curiously. He

123

raised his hand in greeting and they giggled behind their fingers. The men were nowhere in sight.

For another week he saw only the women and very young children. He spent each day walking up and down in front of the tipi, then lifting rocks to strengthen the muscles of his arms and chest, stretching his legs, doing a little more every day, pushing himself to the limit, walking a little farther. The Shoshoni had given him buckskins and moccasins to wear and he found them comfortable. The tribe, or at least the women he saw, accepted his presence after a few days. He wondered where the men were. He suspected they returned every evening, but his body was healing and he found himself falling asleep every evening by nightfall and not stirring until the sun was well up. He did not want to ask about the mysterious absence of the tribe's men and why Istaga had not come to see him. Like most Indians, the Shoshoni did not respond to curiosity. The men would appear sometime. Once, he asked Kimama to give a message to Istaga for him.

"Tell him that he has traded a grizzly bear for my life," Fargo told her. He knew Istaga would understand his message. Fargo had saved Istaga's life. And the Shoshoni had repaid him in kind.

"Oh, the grizzly bear! I have heard this famous story," Kimama said. "Istaga has told it already many times to the children at night around the fire. I will tell him your message."

One afternoon, after he had lifted his daily quota of rocks and walked a hundred times around the village, Kimama appeared beside him. Today she was wearing a dress he hadn't seen before, a white doeskin that clung to her rounded body. The fringe moved with her graceful gait and the beads shone like her long black hair and her eyes.

"Very pretty," Fargo said, pointing at the dress.

"You like?" Kimama took his arm and pulled him through the village. She grinned as if she had a secret. He wondered where she was taking him. Three of the older women were following them at a distance, laughing behind their hands. Kimama led him out of the village and through a grove of wild cherry trees.

Fargo glanced behind and saw the three women still following them. "You sure this is alright?" he asked.

Kimama led him on for another short distance until he heard the sound of running water up ahead. There in the trees, he glimpsed a stream running into a deep pool surrounded by rocks that mostly hid it from view. As they came nearer, he saw that the pool was crystal clear and an extraordinary color, a deep blue at the deep center that faded to a pale shade at the edges, like the trumpet of a morning-glory flower. It almost didn't look real.

Kimama pushed him toward it, and when he came to the edge, she tugged at his buckskin top, indicating that he was to take it off. He complied and she unwound the bandage from his midsection. He looked down to see that the bruises that had been violently purple and red had begun to fade to yellow and gray.

"Good," she said, tracing them with her finger. She pointed at his breeches, then at the water.

"You want me to take a bath?"

He kicked off his moccasins and stuck one toe in the water, surprised to find it very warm. He glanced over his shoulder and saw that the three older squaws were standing a short distance away in the cherry grove with their backs turned. Obviously they were keeping watch. As he stripped and lowered himself into the hot water, he marveled at the subtle way the Indians dealt with certain things. At least things that weren't scalps.

As the water rose up to his neck, the heat radiated through his body, relaxing every muscle, penetrating his limbs and his joints. He seated himself on an underwater rock and lay back, letting himself enjoy it. He heard Ki-mama clear her throat and opened his eyes to see her standing beside the pool. She smiled at him, then reached down and slowly lifted the white doeskin dress to reveal her round legs, the dark triangle of fur between her thighs, her softly rounded belly, and then the two full breasts tipped with dark nipples and areolae. He felt himself harden at the sight of her, saw his cock swell and rise under the water. She threw the dress off and stepped delicately into the pool.

6

Kimama walked slowly through the hot-spring water toward him, her figure outlined by the mysterious morning-glory blue of the deep natural pool. Her nipples were just under the surface of the water, and as she came within his reach, he put out his hand and touched her, cupping his hand beneath the roundness of her softness. He pulled her toward him and she moved eagerly. He felt her hand on his swollen cock, stroking him, exploring his balls, tickling the tender tip of him. He was throbbing with desire.

Without a pause, she opened her legs and lowered herself onto his lap, sliding down over him. He slid into her smooth sheath that was cooler than the hot water around them. He pulled her closer and kissed her, deeply. She pulled his tongue into her mouth, exploring with her own, her hands moving like butterflies over his shoulders, through his hair, across his ears. He started to move up and down, shifting his hips, but she shook her head subtly. Then he felt her contract around his cock, a subtle squeezing like a mild wave. He smiled and she did it again, again. She shifted on him, moving him once in and out, then squeezing him again. He tried to move against her, but she shook her head.

He lay back. Hell, he wasn't going to fight it. He felt

127

the surges of pleasure wash over him as she moved up and down, tightening around him. He squeezed her breasts, flicked his fingers across her tight nipples, and she cried out. His cock grew harder and he felt ready to shoot up into her, but then she slowed and let him retreat from the brink for a while.

He reached his hand down under the water and felt for her, exploring the delicate folds of her, finding the small button of pleasure. When he touched it, she tightened and gasped. He rubbed her slowly, then faster. Kimama's eyes were half-closed, her face flushed with pleasure and her breath coming in gasps. She mumbled words he could not understand, then began to shudder as she moved up and down on him, out of control, her body in a spasm of orgasm.

She moaned and he felt his cock swell even more, felt the urgency, the explosion gathering at the base of him and the contraction, the release, the pumping upward as he shot into her, held her hard against him, moved her up and down on him, in and out, shooting up, again and again, until there was no more and she fell against him. He wrapped his arms around her softness, holding her close, inhaling the pine scent of her hair as she clung to him. After a while she pulled away and kissed him on the chin.

"I think Eagle-on-Wind is no more sick."

"Everything is working again," he said with a laugh.

They lounged around the pool for a while longer, then climbed out. The three older squaws were now sitting down under the cherry trees, facing away toward the village. Fargo wondered how much they'd watched, but he didn't really care. The cool air felt refreshing after the heat of the pool and they were soon dry and dressed again.

Fargo felt refreshed. The hot spring had done him a world of good. Not to mention Kimama. He put his arm around her and squeezed her.

"You like to walk to see special place like man?" She pointed down at his crotch.

"What?" he asked, wondering what she was talking about. She giggled and led him along a narrow trail through some rocks and a short way through a thick pine wood. The three squaws followed behind at a discreet distance. Kimama led him onward, and as they emerged from the trees, Fargo gazed across a bizarre landscape, unlike anything he'd ever seen. Before him was a wide gray plain of solid rock that seemed to have been chiseled in rifts by a giant's hand. Here and there puffs of steam arose from the rock as if it were the breath of some gigantic subterranean monster. The flat gray rock was mammoth and surrounded on all sides by a dark fringe of pine trees. A strange gurgle and hissing sound emanated upward from the earth.

"Land of Noise," Fargo said, remembering Istaga's name for his tribal lands.

"That's right," Kimama said. She stood, looking expectantly across the rock flat.

"What are you waiting for?" Fargo asked her.

She giggled and pointed down again to his crotch.

Suddenly he heard a hissing sound and saw a puff of steam, then a fountain of steaming water spray upward into the air, higher and higher, straight up more than fifty feet. It was amazing. A huge geyser. He had heard about them but had never seen one. Fargo laughed when he understood what Kimama had had in mind and he bent to kiss her. She laughed, too, and pointed to the fountain as it gradually lowered, then spurted and ceased. All was quiet again.

"How did you know it was going to—" He paused and gestured upward with his hand, lacking the vocabulary to say what he meant.

"Every day, like the sunrise," Kimama said. She held up her hands and counted on her fingers to ten, then to twenty and four more. "Every day," she said. "And all night, too."

"Twenty-four?" he asked. She was telling him that the gigantic geyser erupted every hour, all day and all night. He shook his head in wonder. Colter's Hell. Yeah, no wonder folks had a hard time believing Colter's tales. It was pretty amazing, and if Fargo hadn't seen it with his own eyes, he'd have had a hard time believing it.

They walked back to the village and, as soon as they arrived, noticed that all the women were scurrying around like ants. Half the tipis had already been taken down and packed up to be dragged behind the horses and the skins had been removed from the others. As Fargo watched, several women pulled down the tall lodgepoles, which started to teeter. Fargo ran forward and grabbed the heavy tipi supports, then helped the women lower them to the ground.

There was no time to talk and questions were unnecessary. Clearly, the tribe was in danger and the village was being moved. The women bustled about with the efficiency of a trained army unit. Even the small children had assigned tasks like loading the pack animals and rolling up the bedding and tipi skins.

Half an hour later Fargo followed on foot as one of the women led away the last of the pack animals. Kimama fell into step beside him. Even then, he did not ask any questions. Instead, he pushed her up ahead and fell behind her several hundred yards. As they retreated, he kept watch behind them.

Then, a few hundred yards back, he spotted a group of braves. Hoping to find Istaga among them, he waited on the trail until they caught up. When they came nearer, he did not recognize his friend, but the braves expressed no surprise at seeing him. One silently handed him a knife, which he tucked into his buckskin trousers. He continued to walk with them through the forest, following the women as the tribe moved its village to safety.

They did not stop walking until midnight. During the long hours Fargo had occasion to turn his mind back to the events in the small valley. He had been in the Shoshoni village for a full month now. It was hard to believe. But now he was almost fully recovered. And it was time to move on. Time to settle old debts. Time to track Jim Tritt down. He wondered if Doherty and Bethany were still alive, if Tritt had fallen for Fargo's lie and had given up his search. Or maybe he'd dug up the money anyway and was already down in South America, living it up. Fargo thought again of Mike Ford and clenched his teeth until his jaw ached.

By the time they reached the spot where the new village would be set up, the women had already begun work on the tipis. The men Fargo was with began to help with the lifting of the lodgepoles and the stretching of the skins over the tipi frames. Once again, Fargo pitched in. The children had been herded into one of the tipis and told to sleep while the adults finished putting up the shelters. They worked by moonlight and in another hour it was done.

Suddenly someone touched him on the shoulder and Fargo turned to see Istaga in his plaid shirt and buckskins standing beside him. The wide Coyote grin was on his face. They grasped hands.

"Welcome, friend," Istaga said. "Eagle-on-Wind is welcome in the Shoshoni tribe. My sister, Butterfly Woman, is happy since one month to have you join us."

It was a lot of words for a Shoshoni to say all at once.

"I am made new," Fargo said. "Thanks to Butterfly Woman. Thanks to Shoshoni hospitality."

Istaga paused and looked him over with a smile. "Much better since we found you. Looked like butchered bear. Now, come."

He turned and led Fargo to a tipi toward the center of the newly erected village. Fargo had noticed the tipi before; its skins were strikingly decorated with designs of running buffalo, circles, and arrowheads. Istaga bent and entered the flap and Fargo followed.

Inside the tent was a circle of men. A fire burned in the center and Fargo smelled the smoke of the sacred tobacco. A pipe was being passed around. Fargo knew the protocol. When Istaga pointed to a spot on a buffalo robe, Fargo lowered himself and sat cross-legged in the circle of men.

No one spoke for a long time. Fargo puffed on the pipe as it passed around the circle. Then an old man with long gray braids began chanting. Fargo had seen him before and suddenly remembered catching sight of him by the stream, just before he'd been ambushed. The old man caught his eye and nodded gravely in greeting.

"I am Mountain Snow."

Fargo made the customary greeting to the tribe elder, offering the ritual compliments for the tribe's hospitality. Mountain Snow nodded, obviously pleased that Fargo knew the Shoshoni ways. Then he wasted no time getting to the point.

"Why do white men come to our land?"

Fargo considered the question. Many of the tribes had asked him the same question and it was a hard one to answer. Land. Gold. Greed. A new start. How could the Indians understand any of this? Who could explain why the waves of white settlers were pouring into the wilderness? But then he realized Mountain Snow might be asking a more specific question.

"I have been asleep," Fargo said. "My enemies," he said, meaning Tritt and his gang. "Many men on horses. They are still in your land?"

Mountain Snow nodded.

"A woman is with them. She is still alive?"

"We call her Ember Hair," Istaga said with a laugh. The other men chuckled and Fargo felt a wave of relief. So at least Bethany was still alive, but he doubted Tritt had been kind to her. He asked about the old man and found out he was also with the group.

"And the chief must be carried by his braves," Mountain Snow said. "He cannot walk. Someone made a bullet here." The old man pointed at his hip and nodded to Fargo. So Tritt had been crippled by the last bullet Fargo had fired.

"And did you see a horse, a pinto—"

Mountain Snow laughed when he heard the concern in Fargo's voice. "The snow-and-night horse will not let anyone ride on its back," the old man said. "The chief tries, but the horse throws him on the ground. The horse has a great spirit."

Fargo breathed a sigh of relief to know his precious Ovaro was all right. "What do my enemies do?"

"I think they try to find the sun-metal," Mountain Snow said thoughtfully. "For one moon we watch. They move place to place. They dig in the earth like a dog after a badger. Then they go another place and dig again."

Fargo considered this. So Tritt and his gang were still looking for the stash of counterfeit bills. And Tritt had also figured out that Fargo had been lying about the Treasury Department alerting all the banks. But if they were still looking, then something must have gone wrong with the map. Maybe it had been destroyed. Or maybe it wasn't accurate. In any case, they were still looking. And the presence of Tritt in the neighborhood explained the sudden move of the village. It also explained why none of the Shoshoni men and boys had been around during the day. They'd all been off keeping watch on the movements of the white men so the village would not be found and attacked by surprise.

"It is not gold that they are looking for," Fargo said. "They are searching for a big box of—of—" There was no Shoshoni word for money. "Of buffalo skins and horses and beads," he said lamely.

The circle of men talked excitedly for a moment. This was a wonderous thing indeed, they seemed to be saying, a box of skins and horses and beads. One fat old man protested that he did not believe the words of the white stranger. Fargo turned to Istaga for help, asking him to remember the pieces of paper leaves that the white man used for trading. Istaga nodded and explained to the Shoshoni about the idea of money.

"And other men came, many summers ago to this land." Fargo flashed his fingers, ten, twenty, then five. "So many summers ago, they put this box into the land of the Shoshoni. Now these other men come to find it."

The men talked among themselves for a while until they all understood what he meant.

Then Mountain Snow held up his hands and they all fell silent. "I was a young man like my son, Coyote, when the white men brought this box into Shoshoni land," he said. "I did not see inside, but I believe it is the same."

"You know where it's buried?" Fargo asked.

Mountain Snow nodded.

Fargo stared into the fire for a long while, a plan starting to form in his mind. Yes. Yes, it might just work. "I think I can help you get rid of the white men," he said.

Mountain Snow shook his head sadly. "If we kill them, take their scalps, other white men will come to kill us. More white men than all the stars in the sky."

"Not this time," Fargo said.

Mountain Snow reached behind him and brought out an object that glittered in the firelight. Fargo recognized Mike Ford's watch. He snapped it open and saw the picture of the woman's face inside. Ford's girlfriend in Philadelphia. Fargo decided that when all this was over, he'd take the watch back to her. It was the least he could do for Mike. The men stood up and left the tipi one by one. Istaga led Fargo to another tipi and he lay down under a buffalo robe. Sleep came immediately.

He woke with the larks for the first time in a month. He stretched under the heavy robe, feeling the almost pleasant ache of his muscles, the strength flowing again through his body. He rose and walked outside. Many of the women were already up cooking over the fires. A group of young boys were taking care of the horses and they looked at him curiously as he passed by. He spotted Kimama stirring something in a pot, and walked over. She served him a bowl of hot grain flavored with honey. He found he was ravenous and ate a second bowl. The men began emerging, armed with bows and many of them carrying rifles. They ate quickly, some of them mounted horses, and others set off on foot in small groups. Fargo spotted Istaga, who motioned for him to join him. They mounted two saddleless Appaloosas and set off through the woods.

It was good to be on a horse again, but Fargo missed the pinto. For the next several hours they rode through the strange landscape of Colter's Hell, or the Land of Noise. Fargo saw vast pools of bubbling mud like the hot cauldrons of hell. Steam rose in columns from the rocky land. They stopped to look down into still pools whose depths seemed to be carved from green-and-purple marble. In other places, odd rock columns rose high above them, looking as if they were formed of dripping wax. They rode by the site where the village had formerly been located and Istaga took him down by the gray rock flats that Kimama had shown him.

"Is that geyser going to blow?"

Istaga looked at the sun and nodded. "The angry god in the earth spits twenty-four times every day and night."

Fargo pulled Mike's pocket watch out and snapped open the case. In another minute he heard the rumbling and hissing increase and then the geyser blew, once again shooting hot water high into the air. It was an amazing sight. Fargo glanced at the watch face. Ten after the hour.

"The Shoshoni squaws have a saying about this. . . ." Istaga began, then hesitated.

"I've heard it already," Fargo said with a chuckle. They rode on. Istaga led him on a long gallop to the west and they approached the edge of a wide canyon. They dismounted and let the horses go graze. Then they crept forward on foot until they were looking down into a valley below. There, Fargo saw Tritt and his gang.

They were digging beside a streambed. Even at this distance, Fargo could make out the figure of Tritt sitting on a horse. He was consulting a piece of paper he held up before his eyes—obviously the map. Nearby on another horse he spotted Bethany. From the slump of her body, he could tell she was dispirited. Bruno Riker was there, too, a shovel over one shoulder as was Alfred Doherty. In several places in the valley, Fargo could see places where the earth had been dug up, as though graves had been started and then abandoned.

He and Istaga sat down and watched for an hour as Tritt's men dug feverishly in the earth. The hole was as big as a grave and he could see that the deeper they got, the less energetically they dug, losing hope. It was hard to believe that they'd spent a month digging holes all over Colter's Hell, finding nothing, and still they continued. It was amazing what greedy men would do.

Finally, some of the men tossed their shovels into the hole; obviously they had decided to give up on this spot. Tritt pointed at the stream and made one of his men pace out a straight line, then turn right and count out more paces. Tritt rode over to the spot and looked at the map. Then they began to dig again.

Istaga shook his head. "I don't understand white men."

"I don't either," Fargo agreed.

They spent the day watching. Istaga brought out strips of pemmican, pounded dried fruit, and a deer stomach filled with honey-flavored water. While they watched, they talked. Istaga told some tales of the wanderings of his tribe and Fargo told of some of his adventures with the Blackfeet up north. When the sun reached its zenith, Fargo brought out Mike Ford's watch and set it at noon, then wound it up. Istaga listened to it tick with wonder.

By late afternoon, Tritt and his men were fed up. Watching the tiny figures below in the valley, Fargo could only imagine the mood among Tritt's men after the long frustrating month. They knew a fortune was there somewhere if only they could find it. But he imagined that every time they were ready to give it up, they remembered that the very next shovelful of dirt could uncover enough money to make them all millionaires.

The plan Fargo had been formulating was taking clearer shape in his mind. Yes, he could see it all now. Istaga glanced over to see him smiling and clapped him on the shoulder. When Tritt and his men moved out, Istaga and Fargo followed, riding the rim of the canyon to see the white men return to their camp beside a gravel-shoaled river a mile down the valley.

By the time they returned to the Shoshoni village, Fargo knew he was ready to put his plan into action. First, he found Mountain Snow and asked if the old man would lead him to find the box at the next day's dawn. And he needed six braves to help dig it out of the ground and a travois to transport it. Mountain Snow agreed to his request.

Then Kimama helped him find a large deer hide that had been scraped smooth by the women. Using a pointed stick and black dye that the women made from berry juice and charcoal, Fargo began to write a message to Tritt. He smiled to himself the whole time. So his bullet had missed Jim Tritt's heart. He was about to get a third chance at the bastard. And this time he wouldn't miss.

After a dinner of fresh rabbit and a few hours by the campfire, Istaga and Fargo mounted the Appaloosas and left the village. Fargo carried the rolled-up deerskin under his arm. They rode to a point half a mile from Tritt's camp on the river and Istaga stayed with their horses while Fargo went ahead on foot. Yard by yard, he crawled closer until he was hunched down behind a low fringe of sage. Slowly, he rose to his feet and scanned the camp. He doubted anyone would spot him in the darkness.

There was a circle of canvas tents with the horses tethered in the center. It was hardly guarded at all. One man sat on a rock by the red embers of the fire and seemed to be dozing. For a whole month the Shoshoni had watched every move Tritt and his men made and yet the white men didn't even know the Indians were there.

Fargo searched the dark forms of the horses and spotted the familiar black-and-white markings of his Ovaro. The pinto must have caught his scent. It whinnied.

Fargo ducked down behind the sage. The man sitting by the fire started awake, took a turn around the camp once, sat down again by the fire, and was soon asleep. After ten minutes Fargo moved forward. He stole silently up to one of the tents and unrolled the deerskin, draping it over the ridge of the tent with the inked words facing upward. Then he retreated.

As he and Istaga returned to the Shoshoni village, Fargo imagined the uproar that would erupt in the morning when Tritt and his men found that someone had stolen right into their camp. And Tritt would be furious once he read the message written on the skin:

Greetings, Tritt

I've come back from the dead. No kidding. And I've got the treasure. You want it?

Bring Doherty, Bethany, and my pinto to the place indicated on this map at exactly noon tomorrow. Don't come early. Don't come late. We'll trade. And don't try any tricks or you won't get the money.

Skye Fargo. No kidding.

Dawn was breaking as Mountain Snow led a line of Shoshoni on horseback along a high ridge. The old man stopped and pointed down into a grassy meadow below, cut by a brook.

"I was a young man and I sat here and watched the

white man make a hole in the earth and put this box into it," Mountain Snow remembered. "Many summers ago."

They descended the grassy slope and Mountain Snow rode back and forth along the stream, examining the ground. Then he dismounted and indicated a spot.

The braves moved forward and used their tomahawks to break through the thick sod. Fargo joined in as they scooped up the earth with metal tools like shovels without handles. They had only gone down six inches when they struck the top of the box. It was made of metal and it took another hour before they could slide a rope underneath it and hoist it up out of the hole. It was padlocked shut and Fargo used one of the Shoshoni rifles to shoot it open. The Shoshoni huddled around, eager to see inside. The lid came open with a loud squeak.

"Shit," Fargo said. The piles of bills were there all right. Stacks of them. But over the years moisture had leaked into the box and the ink had smudged to the point where nobody would mistake them for real bills.

Fargo swore again. Hell, the plan might fall through. Mountain Snow looked concerned. Fargo lifted a stack of the counterfeits and found that underneath the top layer, the bills were fine. He removed the top stacks of spoiled bills and started discarding them, throwing them into the hole. One of the braves took a bundle from him and examined it. They passed it from brave to brave as each inspected the counterfeit money, holding it up to the sunlight and even smelling it. Istaga looked at it last, then shrugged and tossed it away.

Now Fargo had a nice clean layer of crisp counterfeit bills on the top of the box. He closed the lid and, together with the Shoshoni braves, eased it onto the sturdy travois, then set off, making their slow way to the rendezvous point.

A minute before noon, Fargo snapped open Mike Ford's pocket watch and consulted it again. Almost time. And all was in place. Far across the flat gray rock face, the chest of counterfeit bills stood waiting, so distant as to be almost invisible. There was nothing else in sight—only Fargo, who stood alone on the rock flat waiting. He had changed out of the Shoshoni buckskins and into the tattered and bloodstained clothing that he'd been wearing the day Tritt almost killed him. It was all part of the show.

Then he heard the sound of horses approaching, the hoofbeats, the creak of leather saddles, and the jangle of spurs. In another moment Tritt and his men emerged at the edge of the woods and halted.

Jim Tritt rode out in front, followed by Doherty and Bethany on horseback, their arms tied in front of them. Tritt was taking no chances. Bruno Riker rode off to the right, leading the pinto, and the other men ranged behind. Tritt stared hard at his solitary figure out in the open, as if not believing his eyes.

"Yeah, I'm really alive," Fargo said. "You left me too soon and I crawled away. I've been living off the land and regaining my strength while you've been looking for those counterfeit bills. But I just happened to find them first."

"I don't believe you," Tritt yelled.

"I'm not armed, Tritt," Fargo called back. "I came to do some trading. Money for hostages. And three horses. I just want to get out of here."

Tritt's horse moved forward a few steps and then he motioned for his men to draw their rifles. Looking all around them, Riker and his men ventured out onto the gray rock, skirting the vents of steam rising here and there. Five yards away they stopped. The pack of men was bristling with rifles. And every one of them was trained on Fargo. One false step and he was a dead man.

Fargo took a close look at Tritt. He took some satisfaction from the dark scab that still covered one side of Tritt's skull where his ear was missing. And, more than that, in the thick face, he could see lines of pain. One leg hung loose from the stirrup and Fargo knew the wound he'd given Tritt in the hip had messed him up good.

Bethany's face was drawn and her eyes lusterless. Doherty's white beard was bedraggled and he looked like he'd been through hell as well.

"So, where's the money, Fargo?"

Without another word, Fargo pointed in the distance to the chest, which could be seen on the distant edge of the rock plain.

Tritt looked suspicious. "Take two men and go check on it, Riker," he ordered.

The huge hulking man let go of the pinto's reins, and followed by two of his cohorts, they picked their way across the rock toward the chest. Everyone waited in anticipation as the group warily approached the chest and opened it. There was a yell of glee and the three men began tossing the money in the air. It floated down like autumn leaves.

At that moment Tritt's men gave a roar and all discipline broke down. Even Tritt forgot himself in his haste to get his hands on the money. In an instant they were galloping across the gray rock in a disorderly pack, swarming toward the promised riches they had been searching for. Once there, they dismounted and their horses wandered untethered.

Tritt had to be lifted off his horse and half carried to see the treasure. His men clustered around the chest, each man trying to get the best view, to get his hands around a stack of bills. Tritt's men were dancing about, the counterfeit bills fluttering down like confetti. The rock echoed with their shouts of joy.

Fargo felt the Ovaro's soft nose on his hand and he patted it. The pinto hadn't been curried for a long time and its coat had dulled. He doubted it had been fed well either, but the gleam was still in its eye. It hadn't lost its spirit.

"They're not going to let us get away," Bethany said in a flat voice as she sat on the horse and watched the men go wild in the distance. She was obviously so dispirited, she wasn't even considering escape.

"Let's go now," Doherty said urgently. He struggled to free his hands from the ropes. "What are you waiting for, Fargo? Cut us loose. Let's get out of here."

"No, wait," Fargo said. A moment after he spoke, it began. The rumbling in the earth, the hissing, and then suddenly the geyser blew. The boiling hot water shot up into the air and rained down on Tritt and his men. The horses sped off in all directions, escaping from the water. Some men started after them. Others tugged at the chest, trying to drag it away. In the first instant they howled in surprise, then in pain as the water and steam burned them. The men tried to run, but many of them slipped on the slick rock. Then came yells of rage and Fargo knew the men, stumbling about in the steam, had seen that the water was spoiling the bills, that the ink was running on all of them, making them utterly worthless.

"I'm glad," Doherty said as he realized what was going on. "That's a burden lifted from my soul."

"Get back into the cover of the woods," Fargo said. He swung up onto the pinto, happy to be again sitting astride the Ovaro—the only home he knew. He sat watching the battle. Tritt's men were scattering now, running desperately on foot, retreating from the boiling geyser that continued to shoot high into the air. And just then the shooting started.

From all around the rock, from out of the deep cover of the tall pines, bullets and arrows began to rain in on Tritt and his men. They screamed in surprise and fury. The few remaining horses reared up and screamed. The men leveled their rifles and blasted into the darkness of the forest, returning the fire at their unseen enemy. Around and around they ran in a panic, seeking cover. Some hid behind the bodies of others who had fallen. One man had been lucky enough to snag a horse and he rode slumped across its neck, his body so full of arrows it looked like a porcupine as the horse galloped round and round. The geyser had died down now.

Suddenly a man jumped up from where he had been lying on the rock, pulled the dead man down off the horse, and despite the rain of bullets and arrows, hoisted himself up. He galloped straight toward Fargo. It was Riker, all eight feet of him, bloodied and battered and mad as hell. And he had his rifle trained straight at Fargo.

Fargo felt for his gun and then realized he was unarmed. He ducked just as Riker pulled the trigger, but the shot never came. The rifle had gotten soaked in the spewing geyser, Fargo thought. So they'd be hand-to-hand now. Riker was barreling straight for him and Fargo waited until he'd come close, then he leaped out of his saddle and hit the man in midair. They tumbled off and Riker hit the hard stone first, rolling over, his huge meaty hands grappling for Fargo's neck.

Riker's greasy lanks hung down in Fargo's face as Riker struggled to sit on top of him. Fargo summoned all his strength and delivered a powerful uppercut that snapped back Riker's head. Then another, a right in the jaw. The big man's eyes clouded for a moment and his grip loosened. Fargo broke his arms loose and kneed the man in the belly. The breath left him and Riker gasped.

Then Fargo got wearily to his feet. Riker was kneeling on the rock, shaking his head. Fargo clubbed him with his forearms and Riker suddenly rose up like a maddened grizzly, rushing Fargo. They went down again, rolling over and over, but this time Fargo came out on top. Riker had his huge hands around his throat and he was squeezing. The world began to whirl. With a wave of fury, Fargo grabbed Riker's collar and pulled his head up, then smashed it down against the hard stone, once, twice, three times. Fargo got to his feet. The huge man stared up into the sky, eyes blank, his skull shattered.

Fargo gazed across the rock strewn with bloodied bodies of men. The firing had stopped and the Shoshoni had emerged from the edge of the woods. They were awaiting his signal to begin taking the scalps. Fargo walked slowly among the dead, viewing the carnage. In the puddles of water floated the ink-stained rectangles of paper, utterly worthless. There were pools of blood everywhere, broken arrows, broken bodies.

Finally, he found what he was looking for. Near the sodden chest he found the body of Jim Tritt, lying half in a puddle of water. A bullet had found him and blood seeped out from his chest, staining the puddle a deep red. His eyes were open and in one hand he clutched a wad of the counterfeit bills. Fargo felt a presence beside him and glanced over to see Istaga.

"White men die for this?" the Shoshoni asked.

There was no answer to that question. No answer that made sense. Fargo gave the signal and the tribe rushed forward, the braves to take the scalps, the women and children to strip the bodies of anything useful.

Fargo turned and walked away. He saw Bethany and Doherty coming to meet him, but he waved them off. He whistled and the Ovaro came to him. He led it off the gray rock and into the edge of the pine-scented forest. Then he mounted and rode off to find a hot spring. He just wanted to be alone for a while.

After a few days, he knew, he'd ride on. He'd leave this place far behind him. The Shoshoni would strip the bodies. Vultures and buzzards would come. Then the wolves would carry off the bones. And every hour of every day, the geyser would erupt. And eventually, all the blood, all traces of the battle would be washed away.

LOOKING FORWARD!
The following is the opening
section from the next novel in the exciting
Trailsman series from Signet:

THE TRAILSMAN #181
VENGEANCE AT DEADMAN RAPIDS

1860, in the land some call Arizona,
Where the mighty Colorado River rages
And blood-red rocks hide a secret village
Doomed by an ancient oath of revenge.

He spotted the town from a long distance away. It looked like a few wooden crates somebody had set down and forgotten on the middle of a wide red plain surrounded by buttes. As he came nearer, he counted seven rickety false-fronted buildings standing on either side of the trail. In the middle of main street, if you wanted to call it that, since it was the only street, stood a water pump that was hunched over the long wooden trough like a thirsty, rusted vulture.

His lake blue eyes smarted from the baking heat and the white glare of the long ride through the glittering alkali. Dust lay in the folds of his clothing, coated his face, his hands. His horse walked slowly between the small clutter of board structures, its thick hooves clopping on the packed, dry earth, echoing in the silence of the town. When he got close to the water pump, he saw that next to it, somebody had had the bright idea to put up a sign that read: NOWHERE, POPULATION 14.

He dismounted, pumped fresh water into the trough, and dashed some over his head and neck. While his black and white pinto drank deeply from the trough, he glanced at the warped board buildings that clustered along the street with their dust-dim panes like empty eyes. The biggest building was two stories, its warped siding flecked by peeling yellow paint, its shutters hanging askew. The sign read: WISKEE AN WEMEN. He scrutinized the dozen horses that stood tethered and glittering with sweat outside.

Nowhere. Yeah, that about summed it up, all right. He'd arrived at the town of Nowhere for sure.

The pinto, muzzle dripping, raised its head and shook it as if agreeing with his unspoken assessment. He led the horse and tied it in a patch of shade to one side of the saloon, fed it the last carrot from his saddlebag. Whiskey and women. Yeah, he could use a long drink and some female company. The hinges of the batwing doors creaked in protest as he pushed inside.

The Nowhere Saloon was one big room with a few scattered chairs and tables about as rickety as the building itself. A long, carved bar, nicked and scratched, was topped by a broken mirror and stood along one wall. The bartender, a lanky, bald man with eyes like an old bloodhound, looked up as he entered and continued polishing a glass. The dozen men sitting at two large round tables at the rear laid down their cards and turned around in their chairs. They looked like a rough gang, trail-hardened and hungry as old wolves. One of them, a broad-shouldered, big one with lanks of greasy black hair that hung down to his shoulders and a buckskin thong tied across his brow, pulled his pistol and waved it around.

He'd seen this kind before. One false move, one threatening gesture, and the pack of unruly ruffians would be on him in a second.

Skye Fargo had an iron-clad policy not to seek out trouble. In his experience, trouble found him eventually anyway. And tangling with this pack of bruisers would just delay him from the business at hand. He had a job to finish, and the wad of money in his jacket seemed to be burning a hole in the pocket. Yeah, he'd feel easier when the money was in the right hands and the job was done.

So Fargo took no notice of the dozen men watching as he walked across the wooden floor straight to the bar. But he saw them nonetheless, watching them from the corner of his eye for the least whisper of movement, his hand resting lightly on the butt of his Colt, the muscles of his lean body tensed and wary as a cougar's. He hooked his boot over the bar rail and felt their eyes still on him.

"What'll it be?" The bartender rubbed his bald pate nervously.

"Tequila. Salt."

The bartender pulled up a clear bottle with a white liquid and a long worm soaking in it, the real stuff out of Mexico, and poured a glass and set it down alongside a bowl of coarse salt. The men resumed their card game, and as Fargo swigged the liquor, they glanced warily over their shoulders from time to time.

"Never seen you before," the bartender said. He blinked his bloodhound eyes slowly, then took up another glass and began polishing it on his dirty apron.

"Never seen you either," Fargo answered. The bartender shrugged, then grinned as he caught Fargo's wry smile and the gold coin he slid along the bar. "Name's Skye Fargo."

"The Trailsman," the bartender said, making no effort to hide his admiration. "Well, I'll be. Always wanted to catch a glimpse of you. My name's Sims. I heard tell all about you. I knowed you was somebody special when you walked in. Drinks on the house, Mister."

"Keep it," Fargo said as Sims tried to return the coin. The men playing cards hadn't taken any notice of their conversation, and Fargo doubted they'd overheard the words. It was just as well. He preferred to travel incognito. "Maybe you can help me," Fargo added quietly as Sims poured him another tequila. "I'm looking for a man named Ed Dofield. A sheep man, I think. You know where he'd be?"

"Sure, I know Ed Dofield. He'd be up on his ranch about a day's hard ride north. You follow the Little Colorado River north, then cut across west before it gets to the Big Colorado and the canyon. His spread's east of the badlands and tucked up in those grass hills, just at the lip of the Big Canyon."

"Much obliged," Fargo said. He took a pinch of salt on his tongue, then polished off the tequila. It had been a long trail and a hard ride. Now it was almost over and he was about to deliver the money Ed Dofield had been due for more than thirty years and collect his reward. Another job done. And then he was a free man until the next job. He never knew what the next job was going to be, but one thing was for certain—it always caught up to him in the form of trouble.

The card game was getting louder and more raucous. The bartender took the men a couple of bottles of whiskey, and they called out for a couple more. Two of them began arguing, shouting about an ace of diamonds, and Fargo thought it might come to blows, but then they settled down again. Fargo switched to ale and thought about his next move. The afternoon sunlight lengthened across the floor. He could stay in the town of Nowhere for the night, find a pretty woman, settle in a nice hot bath and a soft feather bed.

"The sign outside says *women*," Fargo said.

"Used to be." Sims rubbed his bloodshot eyes and then rested his elbows on the bar. "Town's seen better days. Used to have three doves—purty ones too, a stage-coach drop, and a sheriff. Now we ain't got none of 'em. Can't even get the mail on a regular basis."

"No sheriff?" Fargo asked. "Ain't that kind of danger-ous?"

Sims pulled his hand out of one pocket and showed Fargo the butt of a pistol. "I keep the law and order in here. But out there"—he nodded toward the door—"it's every man for himself."

No women. That made up his mind. There was no point to staying in Nowhere for the night. Yeah, he'd ride on out, bathe in the Little Colorado River, and sleep under the wheeling stars. He'd just finished his last beer and had decided to leave when the jangle of bridles and the creak of leather reached his ears. Swift footsteps crossed the wooden porch outside, and the batwing doors creaked open.

Fargo turned to see a woman standing in the sunlight, blinking her eyes as they adjusted to the dimness inside the bar. Her hair was pulled back, but the light caught the wisps of blond hair around her face that lit up like a golden haze. She was small with a sturdy build, not heavy but round in the right places, and with piercing brown eyes. She was dressed in an Easterner's idea of Wild West clothes, a fringed buckskin skirt and jacket, and she carried a wide-brimmed hat in her hands.

The men at the card game reacted immediately. Several of them rose from their seats and whistled and clapped. She made her way to the bar, ignoring their catcalls. She hardly glanced at Fargo but addressed the bartender.

"Pardon me, sir," she said. "I'm Paulina Parker. Maybe you've heard of me, read my books. *A Hundred Nights on the Amazon?* Or maybe *Romance on the Nile?*" Sims gaped at her, too stunned to answer, so she went on. "Never mind. I'm trying to find somebody to sell me a boat. You know, for river travel. Like an Indian canoe. Anything like that here in this town?" She had a hint of a Southern accent. Her voice was soft-edged like a little girl's, but Fargo also heard a note of firm determination in it. He glanced at her, taking in the curved lines of her form, the long golden braid of hair hanging down her back, the upturned tilt of her nose. She ignored his look.

Behind her, the dozen men were slowly walking toward the bar, listening to her every word. The big, greasy one with the thong headband was licking his lips. Fargo spotted a man in the front in a stained leather hat who seemed to be their leader. He was a short, wiry fellow with a shock of thick gray hair and eyes too close together. He was grinning ear to ear.

"Canoes," Sims said at last. "Canoes. Sure, lady. At the end of the street, ole Zeke's got a bunch he was trying to unload a few years ago. Got 'em stored out back in a sod hut. Bet he'd be glad to sell them to you."

"Wonderful. Thank you so much," Paulina said. She turned to go and stopped abruptly, surrounded by the men. Fargo's hand was on the butt of his Colt when she suddenly spoke. "Don't fuss with me, boys," she said. She fumbled at her waistband, and suddenly a small derringer was glittering in her hand. The wiry man in front took a surprised step back and held up his hands with a laugh. They were all pretty drunk.

"Why, look here, boys," he said, his speech slow and slightly slurred. "It's a lady spitfire." He doffed his hat with an exaggerated motion. "We were just coming over to introduce ourselves, welcome you to the territory."

"Well, thank you kindly," Paulina said. Fargo saw the derringer waver slightly. Yeah, she was putting up a good show, but she was scared, all right. The bartender was standing back from the bar, watching warily.

"I'm Barnes, Cavell Barnes," the wiry man said, replacing the hat on his head. "And these are my friends."

"I'm Platan Arnez, ma'am," the big headband piped up. He was silenced by a look from Barnes.

"Why don't you just come have a little refreshment with us, pretty lady?" Barnes said smoothly. There was a long silence as the derringer hovered in the air, pointed at Barnes' chest. Fargo calculated the odds. A dozen men, some he could take out, some he couldn't because Paulina was in his line of fire.

"No, thanks, Mr. Barnes," she said. "I'm kind of in a hurry. Another time."

She started to back away toward the door, but Cavell Barnes took a step to follow her, then reached out to the derringer. Paulina drew back and seemed to hesitate about pulling the trigger. Barnes was too quick for her, and in a moment he'd wrested it from her and held it on his open palm.

"Now, ain't this a pretty thing?" he said, speaking to the derringer, then looking Paulina over head to toe. This had gone far enough. Fargo's Colt was in his hand.

"Give the lady her gun back." At the sound of his voice, Barnes and his men turned to stare at him. Barnes spun the derringer in his hand and pointed it at Fargo. The rest of the men drew instantly. Six bullets in his Colt. A dozen men all aiming at him dead center. Yeah, the odds weren't great. It could turn into a bloodbath any moment.

"Says who?" Barnes spat. "We're just getting to know the lady." Behind him, Fargo heard Sims pull up his pistol. So now they had twelve bullets for twelve men. Barnes squinted at them. Paulina's chest was heaving as her breaths came quickly.

"I don't like your manners," Fargo said. For a moment he considered Cavell Barnes' shin, imagined a bullet in it. Yeah, it was tempting to wing him. Or maybe his big toe. But that might start 'em shooting. He decided a warning shot would drive them off.

Fargo pulled the trigger and his Colt rang out, a cloud of gunpowder rising around him. Cavell jumped back an instant after Fargo's bullet nipped a chunk of his leather boot and left a hole in the floor. Fargo vaulted sideways and grabbed Paulina around the waist, pulling her back with him and pushing her down beneath him behind the bar. Where he'd stood an instant before, three bullets split the wood of the bar. Sims had ducked for cover.

"Next time I aim higher," Fargo said, covering them with his Colt. Sims took courage and reappeared alongside him from behind the bar like a prairie dog coming up from his hole. "Now, let's have the lady's gun. And get the hell out." Barnes hesitated and then realized he and his men were yards from any table they might use for cover. Meanwhile, Fargo and Sims could pick them off from behind the bar. The odds weren't in his favor now.

"Sure," Barnes said, tossing it toward him. It landed on the floor and discharged, the bullet flying wide.

"Shit!" one of the men yelled, grabbing his arm. The bullet had grazed his flesh. Barnes ignored the disruption.

"Sure. We're going. But we ain't going to forget this, Mr. Skye Fargo." Fargo exchanged surprised glances with the bartender. Barnes headed toward the door with the rest of his men following and spoke over his shoulder. "Yeah, I know who you are. Recognized you when you walked in, Trailsman. We'll be looking for you. I never forget an unkindness to me and my boys."

The men piled out the door, and in a moment the room was deserted. Fargo helped Paulina to her feet and retrieved her derringer.

"Thank you so much, Mr.—Mr. Fargo, was it?" she said, her manners a little formal but her words sincere. She stuck out her hand and Fargo took it, small in his and cool to the touch. He let it go reluctantly, realizing he was damn hungry for female company. "I'm Paulina Parker. Author. Maybe you've read my books—*A Hundred Nights on the Amazon?* And—"

"Romance on the Nile," he finished for her.

"You have read my books? You've actually read them?"

"No, I just heard you mention them to Sims here," Fargo said. The bartender offered her a drink, and she took a glass of beer. They settled down at a table. "What in hell brings you out here?"

"My next book," she said enthusiastically. *"Down the Raging Colorado.* I'm going to be the first person ever to canoe down the Big Canyon—some folks call it the Grand Canyon. I hear it's one of the wonders of the world. I can't wait to see it and write all about it. It will be my best book ever. Now that I'm this far, all I need is a canoe and some supplies."

"And more lives than a cat," Fargo said. "The whitewater in that canyon will chew you up and spit you out in a hundred tiny pieces. You aim your boat six inches too far in one direction and you're done for, smashed to smithereens on a rock sharp as a bear tooth. There's a reason why nobody's tried going down that river. It's just plain crazy. You want to get somewhere in this territory, you get on a horse and ride there."

"Sounds like you know an awful lot about it," she said, seemingly undaunted by his words. She sipped her beer, pulled the braid over her shoulder, and smiled at him. Damned pretty. "Maybe you could tell me what kind of canoe I need. I was thinking birchbark might be lightest and easier to carry for portage. You know, sometimes you have to carry the canoe around the rapids that are too rough."

"You do know something about it," Fargo said. So she wasn't completely ignorant. But the whole idea seemed lunatic. "Just take my advice and don't try birchbark. That river will snap it like a toothpick at the first rapid. You want a solid wood boat, low and wide with a flat keel to get over the shallows. And get somebody to hammer a sheet of tin"—he pointed up at the embossed tin ceiling—"like that over the bottom. And get a cover, some canvas, over the top, so when the water pours in, you don't swamp and sink. Get some air pockets built in fore and aft, animal stomachs will do, to keep her afloat too. But there's one piece of advice I can give you that is the most important thing, the thing you really ought to listen to—"

"Do tell," Paulina said, taking in his every word.

"Forget the whole goddamn thing," Fargo said. "Forget trying to canoe down the Colorado River. You're going to die trying. And that would be a waste of one beautiful woman."

She blushed at his compliment and turned away for a moment. Damn, she was pretty and an unusual woman with an indomitable spirit. Either that or she was just plumb loco. Maybe a little of both.

"You see, I just *have* to go," she said. "I've been like this all my life. I want to experience everything, try everything, have adventures. I've climbed the pyramids in Egypt. I went on a raft down the Amazon River and saw those wild people who are cannibals and shrink human heads." She shuddered. "We almost didn't get away that time. Another time we tried to cross Canada from Nova Scotia to Alaska, but we got caught by the early snows and had to hole up for the rest of the winter."

"Who's this *we*?" Fargo said. Yeah, he'd thought she was unattached. He'd got his hopes up there for a moment.

"Oh, that's Bishy," Paulina said. "Aloisha Bishy, my traveling companion. He's come on all my trips. He's so helpful." A sudden cloud came over her expression. "He ought to be along. Said he'd just water the horses."

A sound of shouting drew their attention, and Fargo rose and ran out of the saloon, followed closely by Paulina. The street was filled with Barnes's men on their horses, and it was clear the fight had just broken out. The tall headband named Platan Arnez had lassoed somebody, looked like an old man, and was dragging him the length of the street while Barnes and the others hooted and hollered from their horses. The old man was already bloody and battered, and it looked like they were fixing to drag him right out of town behind them.

"Bishy!" Paulina screamed.

Fargo drew his Colt and fired in an instant, the bullet

slicing through the rope. The form of the old man suddenly lay still in the dusty street as Barnes and his horsed men rode on. Fargo fired again and Platan Arnez plummeted forward onto the neck of his horse, clutching his arm. Several of Barnes's men turned and fired back. Barnes shouted something unintelligible but furious, and in another moment they'd ridden out of town.

"Bastards!" Paulina screamed after them. Her derringer was in her hand, but she hadn't fired. She ran toward the figure in the street and Fargo followed, keeping his ears alert in case Barnes and his gang decided to double back and make more trouble.

Paulina knelt down on the ground and cradled Bishy's head in her lap. Fargo loosed the lasso and freed his hands. After a moment the old man came around, rubbed his eyes, and groaned.

"Oh, hell, Paulina," he said as his eyelids fluttered and he saw her face over him. "You get us in the worst messes."

"What happened?" Her voice was tender and angry at the same moment.

"That pack of dogs came out of the saloon and asked me if I knew you. I said I been traveling with you for five years now. Before I knew what was happening, they started sweeping the damn street with my belly."

Fargo gave Bishy a hand to his feet, and they walked him over to the water pump, where he cleaned up, washing the blood and dust off. He wasn't hurt too bad, some nasty abrasions on his hands and a scratch on his cheek, his clothing torn up. Grizzled hair flew about his head like a white cloud, and his long beard hung halfway down his chest. His blue eyes were pale as if faded by the sun, and his skin was weather-rough.

Fargo introduced himself and, at the sound of his name, Bishy sat down on the side of the trough in amazement.

"Well, if that don't beat everything," Bishy said, scratching his head. "I can't believe it. Once again, Paulina Parker's amazing luck." He spoke to her, but nodded his head toward Fargo. "You know, you just happened to run into the best damn trail finder in the West. Knows the ways of the wild as good as redskin. Hires himself out to folks that need help. I was just telling you we needed to get us some help to navigate that Grand Canyon water. And here you go running into the only man in the West that can get us through there alive!" Bishy chuckled. "Damn if that don't beat everything, Paulina. I never seen such luck in one person."

"Wonderful!" Paulina clapped her hands. "A trail finder! I had no idea you were for hire, Mr. Fargo! Oh, this is wonderful, this is perfect!" She clapped her hands again.

"Sorry," Fargo said. "I'm not your man. I'm not a tour guide." Paulina subsided into disappointment at his words and started to interrupt, but he continued. "I don't hire out for adventurers. I don't go taking on trouble for the purpose of helping people risk their lives. I don't do anything just for the hell of it. And I'm not for sale."

"But I could pay you well," Paulina said. "I'll pay you very well. Say, two thousand dollars? My last book made lots of money and—"

"No," Fargo said. "No. And that's final. I don't just

work for money. I have to believe what I'm doing is important. Something that needs doing. Good luck getting down the Grand Canyon, but I won't be a party to going off on some kind of whim, getting yourself killed for nothing."

"My books aren't nothing!" Paulina snapped. She wheeled about and stalked off toward two horses tethered beside the saloon and began pulling some things out of her saddlebag.

"She's got a lot of spunk, ain't she?" Bishy said as the two of them watched her march toward a small battered building with a faded sign that read THE GRAND HOTEL.

"Sure has," Fargo said.

"And she's the luckiest person I ever knew," Bishy said, shaking his head. "Why, if I told you half the things I been through with her, you'd call me a damn liar to my face. Rampaging cannibals chasing us through a jungle. A Turkish sultan kidnapping her for his harem. A hundred spear-carrying Watusis on the warpath in Africa. She's just got that knack of getting out of a tight spot. Every time she gets in trouble, some damn thing always happens and she gets out by the skin of her teeth. And then on she goes getting herself into more trouble. I never seen anything like it in my life."

Fargo grinned to himself. Interesting woman, he decided. Spirit, fire, beauty, intelligence. Good combination. Too bad she'd got her mind set on committing suicide trying to run the rapids of the Colorado River.

She reappeared at the doorway of what was called the hotel and called out, "Come on, Bishy! We're going down here to a man named Zeke to get us a canoe. I got us rooms for tonight. We'll set out tomorrow."

Fargo watched her walk down the street, followed by Bishy. She didn't look back. He patted the wad of money in his pocket, thinking of the day's ride north to Ed Dofield's Circle D Ranch, the job he had to finish, thinking of the cold-water bath he'd promised himself in the little Colorado River, of the chill, clear night air as he would sleep under the stars. Get a move on, he told himself. He walked into the hotel.

He carried out a conversation with himself the whole time he signed the hotel register, ordered a hot bath sent up, took the keys to his room, and went to hunt down a good stable for the Ovaro. Maybe, just maybe, he told himself as he brushed the trail dust from the pinto's gleaming coat, he could talk Pauline Parker out of this crazy plan of hers. Or find some other way to persuade her not to get herself killed. Some method of persuasion they'd both enjoy. There was more than one way to save a life.

Paulina seemed genuinely glad to see him when he appeared that evening in the saloon and had clearly forgotten her last angry words. She was still dressed in the buckskins but now had on a red shirt and had loosed her golden hair, which fell over her shoulders in sinuous glittering waves. He'd taken a nice long soak in a hot tub and changed into fresh Levi's and a denim shirt. Much as he hated towns, civilization did have a few advantages. But in the town of Nowhere, the food wasn't one of them.

For the next hour, he dined with Paulina and Bishy on steaks tough as saddle leather, soggy potatoes, and rot-gut coffee. The apple pie was sour. Sims apologized for the food, explaining they didn't get supplies through very often.

Throughout the evening Fargo was on edge, listening for any sound of men on horseback, wondering when and if Cavell Barnes and his men would ride back into town. Barnes said he'd be looking for Fargo, said he'd not forget. And over the years he'd seen a lot of men like Cavell Barnes. They didn't forget.

By the time they'd finished the meal, Bishy excused himself. He was bruised and sore from his encounter with the Barnes gang and eager to sink into a feather bed and give his old bones some rest. He limped off. Fargo ordered two brandies. Sims dug around behind the bar and came up with a dust-covered bottle. He poured two glasses of the honey-colored liquor. Fargo raised his glass to Paulina, then took a sip. He knew fine brandy when he tasted it, and he smiled with pleasure.

"Yeah, this makes up for the meal. It's the real thing," he said. "French. From around the Cognac region. Aged in oak maybe seven years or so. You can taste oak, but it's subtle. It's just right. Perfectly balanced." He swirled it in the glass, took another sip, and sucked some air into his mouth to enjoy the complex fumes.

Paulina summoned Sims and asked to look at the bottle. She looked up from reading the label, her brown eyes full of appreciation.

"Exactly right," she said. "I like a man who knows what he's talking about. No bullshit—if you'll excuse my language." There was a silence as she regarded him across the table. He reached across and took her hand, raised it to his lips and kissed the palm. Her skin smelled sweet, some kind of spring flower he couldn't place. Violets maybe? Startled, she withdrew her hand.

He ignored it and took another sip of cognac, then asked her about her adventures. Two hours later, they were still talking. She'd been a lot of places, for sure, seen a lot of the world and braved a lot of dangers, all because she wanted to be a world-famous author. She saw the trip down the Grand Canyon as her big break. That's why she wanted to go so badly.

"But what about you?" she asked. "I'm sorry I didn't recognize your name, but Bishy tells me you're really famous. He says everybody in the West knows you. Why don't you write a book about your adventures?"

"I'm too busy having 'em," Fargo said. "I like to live my life, and I don't need to tell other people about it." Paulina subsided into silence, and Fargo thought he might have offended her. "But everybody's got a different reason to do what they're doing," he added.

"Why *do* you do what you're doing?" Paulina asked. "This trailblazing, this wandering? Why do you do it?"

Fargo had asked himself that question many a time. It was impossible to explain to her in words the way the land pulled at him, the way the open trail lured him, the joy he felt with the trusty Ovaro galloping beneath him. It was impossible to tell her how the mountain peaks spoke, called to him. How a lone eagle floating in the blue sky seemed to be a sign to ride on through the miles of dark forests, waving grasslands, searing desert. Something told him that someday civilization would spread throughout the West, that the little settlements would become towns and then cities, would fill the wild lands and roads would crisscross it like so many ropes. Some people said the West would never be tamed, but Fargo knew in his heart that they were kidding themselves.

And then there were the troubles that found him—the father whose daughter was taken off by *banditos*. The town overrun by a gang of no-goods. A woman in search of a treasure so she could save a mission orphanage. A tribe of Indians being cheated out of their hunting grounds. A family held hostage. Yeah, trouble always found him. He came out of his reverie to realize she was studying his face as if she could read his every thought.

"I understand," she said, and Fargo knew she did. They had something in common. She had her adventures for her reason and he for his. But in some way they were alike. He reached for her hand and she gave it reluctantly. He stroked it with his fingers, lightly, promising more. Her brown eyes were wide, and he read something there.

"You're scared, aren't you?" he said. Paulina swallowed and blushed.

"No."

"Yes," he said. "Yes, you are scared. You said you like experience. You're always looking for adventure." She tried to remove her hand from his grasp, but he held onto it.

"It doesn't include that kind of . . . of adventure."

"Why not? It's part of enjoying life." He let go of her hand. She put both hands in her lap, out of his reach.

"It's like this brandy here," Fargo said, taking another sip and rolling it over his tongue. "The more you know about it, the more experience you have of it, the more you appreciate the really good stuff."

He saw her eyes widen as she took this in, and he wondered if she was a virgin. Maybe, despite all her adventures, she'd never even enjoyed the pleasures of the body. It was possible.

"I think it's time to go," Paulina announced, standing up suddenly.

Fargo paid Sims for the dinner and drinks and followed her out the door. The town of Nowhere was dark and still. Countless stars glittered overhead in the cold and clear desert night, seeming close enough to touch.

"How beautiful," Paulina breathed as she stood in the dark street looking up at them. A coyote barked nearby and she jumped, huddling close to him. He laughed and put one arm around her, felt her stiffen a little at his touch and then slowly relax as he made no further move.

To the east, he saw a pale glow in the sky. Almost moonrise, always a spectacular moment in the desert night. "Got something to show you," he said, walking her to the eastern edge of town.

They stood waiting in the cold night breeze, looking expectantly toward the horizon. The desert night was full of small noises, the yip of the coyotes, distant song of a lone wolf and flap of a bat overhead. They heard a two-note coo, the night call of the burrowing owl. He identified all the sounds for her. Then, between two buttes, the edge of the moon appeared, a white dome that grew swiftly larger, flooding the desert with a light that seemed almost blinding, a huge milk white moon, mysterious and pocked. It rose above the horizon and she shivered. He drew her close, and she glanced up at him.

Then his mouth was on hers, and her lips, shy, hesitant, opened to take his tongue in, her sweetness like honey. He caressed her back as she clung to him, opening to him, hungry, and he felt her loneliness, her want. His hands tangled in the surges of her silken hair, and he kissed her again, again, bent to kiss her neck, inhaling the violet sweetness of her, enjoying the warm softness of her curved hips and back beneath his hands. Suddenly she withdrew, pulled away from him.

"I think I'd best be getting back," she said stiffly. She wouldn't look at him or take his arm. They walked back to the hotel in silence. He followed her up the creaking staircase and down the hallway. A flickering oil lamp stood on a small table next to the door of her room. The key was trembling in her hand so much that she couldn't put it into the lock. He took it from her, inserted it into the keyhole, pushed open the door, and then stepped back. She'd have to invite him in. But she stepped through the door and didn't look back.

"Good night, Skye." He heard the note of regret in her voice, and without meeting his gaze, she shut the door behind her. And locked it. For a moment he stood listening to the creak of her footsteps inside the room as she got ready for bed.

He thought up a string of silent curses. There was no understanding women. He blew out the oil lamp. Moonlight poured through the window at the end of the hallway as he made his way to his room. He hadn't forgotten

Barnes and his gang. All night he'd been on edge, listening and watching, even as he'd enjoyed Paulina's companionship. And before he opened the door to his room, he stood listening, just in case some of those bastards had sneaked back into town and were waiting to jump him. He opened the door wide, but there was no one inside.

The silvery moonlight lay across the white coverlet of the brass bed. He stripped down to the skin, stowed his Colt beneath his pillow, and eased his long, muscular body between the sheets, enjoying the coolness of the fresh cotton, the pillowy soft cloud of the thick feather bed beneath him.

He had almost drifted into sleep when he heard the floorboards creak, a door open. He was alert in a moment, his hand under the pillow reaching for the Colt. There was a light tap at his door. He pulled the bedsheet around him and opened it to find her standing there dressed in a white nightgown with ruffles at the high neck and long sleeves. Her golden hair cascaded down her shoulders, her eyes were lowered, and he saw she was trembling.

"I am scared," she said.

He pulled her gently inside and shut the door behind her.

"This adventure won't be dangerous," he said. "And you'll enjoy it. I promise."

WAR EAGLES
BY FRANK BURLESON

In the North, a lanky lawyer named Abraham Lincoln was recovering from a brutal political setback. In the South, eloquent U.S. Senator Jefferson Davis was risking all in a race for governor of his native Mississippi. And far to the Southwest, the future of the frontier was being decided as the U.S. Army, under Colonel Bull Moose Sumner, faced the growing alliance of Native Americans led by the great Mangus Colorados and determined to defend their ancestral lands. For First Lieutenant Nathanial Barrington it was his first test as a professional soldier following orders he distrusted in an undeclared war without conscience or quarter—and his test as a man when he met the Apache woman warrior Jocita in a night lit by passion that would yield to a day of dark decision . . .

from SIGNET

Prices slightly higher in Canada.   (0-451-18090-9—$4.50)

WHISPERS OF THE MOUNTAIN
BY TOM HRON

The Indians of Alaska gave the name Denali to the great sacred mountain they said would protect them from anyone who tried to take the vast wilderness from them. But now white men had come to Denali, looking for the vast lode of gold that legend said was hidden on its heights. A shaman lay dead at the hands of a greed-mad murderer, his wife was captive to this human monster, and his little daughter braved the frozen wasteland to seek help. What she found was lawman Eli Bonnet, who dealt out justice with his gun, and Hannah, a woman as savvy a survivor as any man. Now in the deadly depth of winter, a new hunt began on the treacherous slopes of Denali—not for gold but for the most dangerous game of all....

from **SIGNET**

Prices slightly higher in Canada.   (0-451-187946—$5.99)